I0556134

DEADLY
ILLUSION

DEADLY ILLUSION

BY ALAN LEBOEUF

DEADLY ILLUSION

Published by Alan LeBoeuf, Edmonton, Canada

ISBN:
    Paperback   978-1-7782163-1-2
        ebook   978-1-7782163-0-5

Publication assistance by

PUBLISHING
PageMaster.ca

If you see a heart.
You should see red
If you see it black
You might be dead

Contents

1

NICE LEGS

If this had been a Raymond Chandler novel, I might have described Marie Dionne as a real cool dame who slid into the chair opposite as easily as a gin and tonic would slide through her ruby-red lips. A sophisticated blonde with long, nyloned legs that seemed to go on forever. But this was not a Raymond Chandler novel, it was the middle of the COVID-19 epidemic, and this was not Los Angeles but Calgary, Alberta. That's in Canada if you don't know it. And this was not sweat dripping down the walls, but condensation from the hot-water pipes you could see through the false ceiling. It was cold in this office. Marie Dionne might have been everything Chandler might have described, but who was to say? She was buried in a thick parka with a designer face mask and goggles. You might wonder about the goggles, but some doc in the States had said that we should all wear goggles because of the virus. Something about mucosal surfaces, he said. So Marie looked like a cross between a bank robber and a mutant from War of the Worlds. I half expected her hand to drop off when we shook hands, but social distancing and all that stuff meant we never touched.

Of course, I wasn't wearing a mask. Too many years of chain-smoking and developing emphysema meant I had a medical exemption. Not officially, of course, but if you heard me cough, you would have no doubts about it. People never bother to ask. This was my first consultation in weeks, so I had overdosed on the cough suppressant. So, who was Marie Dionne, and for that matter, who was I?

My detective agency was called Lou Diamond Investigations, not that this moniker was my real name. Lou Diamond sounded a darn sight better than Sidney Arbuckle, Private Eye. Besides, if you looked up Sidney Arbuckle, you would discover one or two dark secrets. I used to be a cop and if you don't mind me saying so, I was good at my job. Not good enough to merit a TV program, but I have solved a few murder cases. Most, of course, solve themselves.

I got into trouble when I was giving evidence in court one day. I didn't realize it, but my fly was open. Not just a little bit, I'm afraid. The judge was not impressed, or perhaps he was. You never know these days. He found me in contempt, and that was just the start of my troubles. The police investigation followed, and they interviewed my ex-wife. She said "Oh, Sidney's always doing that" and that was that. I lost my job. There was no sentence, but when the judge found out that I was an anti-vaxxer, he ordered me to take a 12-step program that had just been set up. My name is Sidney Arbuckle and I'm an anti-vaxxer. You get the idea. I'm supposed to contact my support link when I get bad thoughts about Bill Gates.

The pandemic had been bad news for many in my business, but I had been lucky. I had a contract to surveil this rich dude in the Pump Hill area of Calgary. His wife thought he was having it away with his partner. Bad enough, I suppose, if it had been a woman. It wasn't. I think they call it non-gender specific, but while I don't give a shit about this sort of thing, this would not go down well in society circles. If you hadn't already guessed, Pump Hill is not the sort of place you went next door to borrow a cup of sugar. This was an enclave for the elite. This dame contracted me to do surveillance. Since we were all in lockdown, I wasn't going to waste much gas on this. I simply parked down the street and watched the minutes go by and the dollars go up. After all, a contract is a contract. And I did have a few mouths to feed, but I'll try not to say any more about my ex-wives.

Most people think that surveillance is easy. You just have to sit and watch and make sure that no one notices. This was difficult for

Red and me. True, we could both blend into most locations, but Pump Hill was a bit different. Then again, we were a lot different.

I know we could look a bit on the rough side, but it wasn't us, it was our security vehicle. It was Red's idea. He thought a converted ice cream van with Walid's Falafels on the side would be the perfect vehicle. Perhaps in an industrial area, it would have worked, but not in Pump Hill. One night there was a flashing of blue lights and here came the boys in blue. I think they were taking the piss, but they asked if we were still doing falafels. I'll be honest, I had no fucking idea what a falafel was, and let's face it, I hardly looked like a Walid. I told them the city had shut us down because of health concerns. Mine. A couple of minutes coughing saved the day and then they buggered off to find the nearest Tim Horton's. That's our local coffee shop in Calgary. It certainly wasn't to be found in Pump Hill. In the end, my client requested I stop the surveillance, but she would keep paying me. She said that our presence was seriously lowering property values in the area.

I just mentioned Red, so I had better let you know who he is. He's the brains of the organization, not that he would ever admit to such. Red, not his real name, was born in Wetaskiwin on the reservation. A tough place to grow up and Red used what came naturally to escape the Res. He became a professional wrestler with Pioneer Wrestling. And he was good until he got injured. Some people suggested it was the steroid use that did him in. But the closest he had ever come to steroids was in his eczema ointment. No, to be fair, he just had a bad shoulder as well as a bad complexion. But he was a pussycat albeit a six-foot-eighteen, 250 lbs. pussycat. I said Red was not his real name. He had so many names when he was wrestling, but I think he was originally called Running Bear, which, let's face it, was not quite the moniker that I needed after my conviction. Just think about it. Running Bear. Nah, don't even bother.

Red and I had been together for 2 years. And never a cross word, well, almost never. About nine months ago, I found out he was drilling my common law, Debra. But we were on the rocks. I knew it was over when she insisted on social distancing. I thought she meant six feet. She meant sixty miles. I took the hint. There were some obvious signs that I ignored. Perhaps I just didn't care. One night there was a half-bottle of whiskey on the coffee table; I hasten to add anything to do with Red. He didn't drink. It was the eagle feather on my pillow. That should have been the big clue. I asked her about it. She said she had been plucking, at least I think that's what she said.

Red and I had words eventually, but it was all quite amicable. He admitted it had been going on for a few months. I told him I sympathized with him and even sent him a thank-you card. It was his problem now. I knew it would never work out with them and it didn't. By the time the card arrived, the affair was over. He's still a lady's man, but I give him a bit of fatherly advice from time to time before he does anything stupid. But he doesn't play the field even if he is what the ladies would describe as being a bit of a hunk. His girlfriend, Jennifer, obviously thinks so. I think the feelings are mutual, but he always asks for my advice. And I'll always ask for his.

Three months ago, he gave me the thumbs up to start dating Rita. A great woman, at least it seems that way after three months. Not perfect. She had incurred a spinal injury when she was pole dancing. It seems that the pole broke, but it was not without its benefits. The lawsuit for damages saw to that. No, she was everything I needed in a woman, and besides, she owned a house that was nearly mortgage-free. I moved in. Oh, and she let Red live in our basement suite. Not that it was palatial, it was a 1950s bungalow that was beginning to look its age. Two bedrooms upstairs and a basement downstairs. The furniture looked as old as the house. But it was home and we, I mean Rita and me, kept it neat and tidy.

Rita and I got on very well. Our backgrounds were so similar. She had been married three times but always seemed to marry just the wrong person. And she did that before she was thirty. She had given up on men. And who could blame her? She was always a hard worker. Her husbands weren't, and that was the problem.

Perhaps some of her issues stemmed from her tough upbringing. Her father deserted the family when she was in her infancy. They had moved around the country several times and she never seemed to have a fixed base. But some people are quite resilient. And Rita was. While doing a menial job, she trained to become a nurse, and I bet she was darn good at it. And then came her injury, but she was the sort of person who argued that I can be in pain and feel depressed or I can do something and feel less depressed. It worked for her.

So that was who we were. That was our team. A group of very different individuals and we were about to get involved in a situation that could only strengthen our ties.

2

THE GREAT BOUDIN

I rarely got cold calls for business, so was a bit surprised to hear from Mme. Dionne. At least, she described herself as Mme. I wasn't so sure. Her French accent was straight out of a soap opera. Sure, it sounded French, but it wasn't. Not that I was an expert on this sort of thing, but I had spent my early years in Montreal, so I knew a French accent when I heard it. I wondered what the game was, but she was willing to pay and for that, she could have come with a Swahili accent. But I had other suspicions. She told me on the phone that I had been recommended and that she had found my number on the internet. Very suspicious. My website had been described as being under construction for a year. But it was a paying gig, so I wasn't about to ask questions. But as sure as hell, I wasn't going to accept a cheque from this dame.

We had arranged to meet at 9.30 on a Monday morning and, unusually, I was on time. She was not. She had been there for 20 minutes and was pacing the corridor outside my office. Made me feel uncomfortable. Being early suggested to me she was just too anxious to tell me her story. And she was. I told her she could sit outside for a couple of minutes. That wasn't good enough. And she wasn't too impressed with Red. She made that obvious. That was sort of understandable. Red was never a picture of sartorial elegance at least at that time. He never had been. I didn't employ him for his looks. I employed him because he could lip-read. And why was that important? I was partially deaf. Too many shots to the head when I was a kickboxer. I quit in my last fight when I said I couldn't hear the bell. A great excuse. I just decided that having the shit kicked out of me was not a good plan.

I escorted Mime Dionne into my office and asked her to make herself comfortable. This was not easy. My office could probably be described as minimalist. An alternative term would have been scruffy. She sat in the only comfy chair I had. Once she had wiped it down, I introduced her to Red. He was sitting on a stool behind me. I described him as my chief forensic investigator. I knew it was bullshit. She knew it was bullshit, and I thought Red was going to piss himself laughing. But it was an opener.

They say that first impressions are the most important ones. I hoped I was wrong. This woman seemed pretentious. She almost acted as if she was too good for this place, which I suppose realistically would not have been difficult. She stared at me for a moment. I said nothing. I always like them to make the first move. It's their story.

"Mr. Diamond, do you mind me calling you Lou." Remember this was said in a false French accent. I am not very good at mimicking bad accents, so use your imagination.

"I'm afraid I do, Marie."

"So, it's Mr. Diamond, I suppose?"

"Nah, just call me Sidney, mam. Sidney Arbuckle,"

"But..."

"Sidney, mam......er, Lou Diamond was my father." Well, I had to say something. Red had to say nothing at all, but he did.

"He was adopted" It explained the difference in name, I suppose.

"Look, what can we do for you?' I said.

"Possibly nothing."

This was not what I wanted to hear. There's not much profit in nothing.

"But I think my husband's life is in danger," she said abruptly.

This was more like it. Even though it could have been delusional, and it usually was, it could take many hours to prove it, and that meant money.

"What makes you think that?" I replied.

She immediately picked up her handbag. It looked Gucci. Probably a knockoff.

"I think this will provide an answer." She took out a rather crumpled piece of paper and passed it to me. I passed it to Red not because I couldn't read but because I had sat on my reading glasses the day before and the glue had not set as yet on the repair. Red started to read the note.

'There are going to be consequences for your treachery, Boudin. Stealing another man's ideas to feather your own nest. This is a warning. You can make a man disappear easily, but it could happen to you, and it will. I won't give you another warning. Plagi.....plagia....' Red stuttered.

"Plagiarism. It means stealing someone else's ideas," she interjected. She said this in a distinctly superior tone. This would not go down well with Red. I knew 15 love would soon become 15 all if this irritated him.

"I know that madam," he replied. "So, do you have any idea who sent it?"

"A few suspicions," she answered.

"Before we go any further," I said, "Who the hell is Boudin?"

"Come, come gentleman. You mean you have never heard of the Great Boudin: the silent illusionist?" she asked.

I turned to Red. "You heard of this guy, Boudin? Now, I could tell that he knew, but he wasn't going to admit it. I could tell he was irritated."

"Rings a bell. Is it used cars? Yes, that's it. The House of Boudin previously enjoyed luxury cars," he said with a wry smile. I knew he was taking the piss. Fifteen all. Time to get things back on track.

"So, tell me who this somewhat famous guy is?" I said.

"I hope you're not being sarcastic, Mr. Arb....Arb." The first sign of some irritation.

"Arbuckle. But call me Sidney. And no, I'm not being sarcastic."

"Pierre Boudin is my husband and has been for many years," she said. "He has been a pioneer in the field of illusion for over 25 years. You could mention him in the same breath as Copperfield, Henning, Burton. Some have described him as the next Houdini."

"Similar name to Houdini. I hope he's that good," I said. " Is that his real name?"

"I'm not sure that is relevant. Would you know who David Kotkin is?" she queried.

"I would," Red said. "That's David Copperfield."

"What the......," I uttered. "How did you know that?"

"I've always had an interest in magic and prestidigitation. It was a great way to pull birds when I used to drink," he said.

"So, you know who my husband is, Mr. Arbuckle?" she mused.

I didn't, but I nodded and smiled as if I did.

"Just a minute," said Red. "It's coming back to me. Wasn't he the winner of "Now You See It" in the States? Now I remember."

"What the fuck is 'Now you see it'?" I said.

Red smiled.

"Don't you ever watch TV, boss?"

"Rarely," I muttered. "I gave up on TV years ago. The only thing I watch now is the Weather Channel."

"It's a program where illusionists make people disappear," he replied.

"Did the show ever feature politicians? That might be a good idea." I thought I was being funny. I wasn't. Dionne fixed me with an icy stare. I thought I'd get her to talk some more.

"Tell me a bit more about your husband," I said. "Sounds interesting."

"My husband was always ahead of his time, but he was a student of the history of magic. Others tended to copy him. That Copperfield was so derivative," she said. There was a bit of spite in that comment.

"Derivative," I queried. "What do you mean?"

"Copperfield became famous for moving the Statue of Liberty and passing through the Great Wall of China."

"I saw it on TV," said Red.

"But it was all so derivative. Pierre had done these illusions before Copperfield. He had moved the Eiffel Tower and passed from one side of the Berlin Wall to the other." I mean, there was a part of me that wanted to ask why the fuck would you even try.

"That was amazing. Ahead of his time, if you don't mind me saying," said Red. She didn't mind at all. She smiled. Perhaps we had broken the ice.

"He was bloody lucky that he wasn't shot if he went through the Berlin Wall," I said. I thought I was being funny again. Course, I always think I'm being funny. She didn't think so...again. She glared. The ice was reforming.

"Mr. Arbuckle, are you going to take this seriously? I could go elsewhere," she asserted.

"Yes, you could, but we are a very economic option here. I want to assure you we have an unparalleled history of success both here and across the province." Of course, it was all bullshit. "So, let me sum this up. You received this letter threatening your husband. And it would appear that it came from somebody who felt that he had......what was the word?" I looked at Red.

"Plagiarized."

"Somebody who felt Boudin had plagiarized his special effects."

"That's right," she said.

"Isn't there legal recourse for this sort of thing?" I replied.

She smiled. "You might think so, but you can't patent tricks and special effects. Illusionists have been copying their peers from time immemorial. They often improve on them. For example, sawing a woman in half has now morphed into sawing the woman into four."

"So, who is this man, and I am assuming it's a man?" She nodded.

"That may be up to you to find out," she replied.

"But you must have some idea who this is. Unless they are delusional, you must have been associated at some time. Have you any ideas?"

"Mr. Arbuckle, I don't want to accuse anyone but...... " Of course, she wanted to accuse someone. That was why she was here.

"We can't go any further if you don't tell me," I demanded.

"OK," she replied. "I think it is someone who used to work for us. Eric Horsfall. We used him to construct some of our effects. He was a good worker, but when we found evidence of cocaine abuse, he had to go. When you deal with illusions, that could be dangerous. Anything that could compromise a performance is simply not acceptable."

"I am slightly confused about this. Why isn't your husband complaining about this?"

"He doesn't know," she said.

"He doesn't know. Don't you think he should? It's his life that's being threatened."

"Look, Mr. Arbuckle, my husband is a very sensitive individual. He is a constant worrier. I don't want anything to disrupt him."

"And he'll be completely insensitive if this Horsfall character carries out his threats," interrupted Red.

"I try not to think about such eventualities."

"Why have you not reported this to the police? And why come to us?" he continued.

"I did. They didn't seem that interested."

"Look Marie, let's get to the point. How can we possibly help you?" I said.

"You could find this man."

"And then what?"

"I think you would agree it would be better if we knew where he was and ....and..."

"And what?" I said.

"Whether this man is dangerous. Does he have a criminal record?"

"I suppose we could do that." I was not about to kiss off an easy-paying assignment.

"Any way that you could just dissuade him."

"We don't do threats," I said. "And we don't do counselling."

"Possibly a bit of gentle persuasion?" Red noted.

"Good. That just might do the trick. So, is there anything you need from me?" I thought I would leave the issue of the retainer for a few more seconds.

"Yes, I need your contact information. I have your cell phone number. I need your address."

"It's all here on my card. I am renting a house in Pump Hill but my, I mean our workshop, is just off Blackfoot Trail. It's all here on my card." Pump Hill again, I thought. Very interesting. Probably just a coincidence. I didn't ask her if she had seen Walid's Falafels on the street.

"There are a couple of other things I need," I said. "The envelope in which the threatening message came in. I'll need it." She took it out of her handbag and passed it to me.

"Anything else?" she said.

"I'll need a retainer. Nothing too excessive for now. We're very economical."

"We'll start at a thousand dollars," said Red. Shit, I thought. A thousand dollars. That's not economic. I would have accepted five hundred. I'd been living off my Tim Hortons card for the last two weeks.

"That seems acceptable, gentleman," she said. "Would you prefer cash or a cheque?" I would have accepted it in Aeroplan Miles.

"Cash," replied Red. "And I will, of course, provide you with a receipt." She opened up her bag and took out a wad of notes and passed it to Red.

"A thousand dollars, Mr. Arbuckle. There's no need to count it." I mean, who the fuck carries a thousand dollars of cash around with them? Of course, I wasn't going to count it. I'm not much good after fifty, but I knew Red would count it. I deflected her attention.

"So, if we find this guy and use a bit of gentle persuasion, any chance of a bonus?" Nothing ventured and all that, I thought to myself.

"Let's put it this way," she said. "Find him in the next week and there will be a substantial bonus." I didn't bother to ask what substantial meant.

She stood up, patted down her clothes, and disinfected her hands with the hand sanitizer on my desk. We hadn't used it in a while. It was beginning to congeal.

"Gentleman, I want to thank you in advance for your efforts. I hope we will be in touch soon." With that, she turned and left the office. No pleasantries. Nothing. I turned to Red. He was sniffing the odour of a thousand crisp banknotes.

"What do you think?" said Red.

"A nice start," I replied. "I'll write the cheque out for Walid tonight."

3
WHO IS ERIC HORSFALL?

I spent that evening chowing down on a takeaway prawn curry. We had a deal with the Chinese takeaway across the street. I watch their premises from time to time. We got an all-you-can-eat invite once a week after a couple of months. Rita was out with her sisters. Prawn curry was as close to a celebration as we could get. Red downed a non-alcoholic beer. As a show of support, I sipped on a hot chocolate from Tims. We turned up the heat. It was late August and snow showers had been forecast. Yeah, I know it was still summer, but I've seen snow every month of the year in Calgary.

Our first task was to discover as much as we could about Pierre Boudin. We started with Wikipedia. Not that it's always accurate, but it gives you a rough idea. There wasn't a lot about him and nothing which matched his wife's description. It described him as being born in Paris in 1987 and being influenced by the great illusionist Robert Houdin. It also showed that he had studied for many years with Doug Henning, the famous Canadian illusionist. That was odd. Doug died in 2000. I'd known him. Boudin would have been 13. Perhaps he had just read Henning's books. But there is no doubt that he had lived for years in Canada. It seemed as if his salad days were about 15 years ago when he enjoyed his 10 minutes of fame. He even appeared on The Letterman Show. He actually made Letterman disappear. Not a bad thing when you think about it. But, I had the impression that his career was in a bit of a downtrend. Then again. Magic and illusions had seen better days. Probably too many exposés on the internet have made everybody an expert. No use watching if you know how it's done.

We looked for Eric Horsfall in the usual places. Facebook, Linked In. You get the idea. Just the sort of places Marie could have looked. Odd that she didn't bother to do it herself. Perhaps she knew that there was not much to find.

We did have one ace in the hole. The Calgary Police Force. I called my contact Louie, who was about to retire. We called him. He would occasionally give me information so long as I didn't expose him as the source. He was at the casino. Said he was there undercover, but we both knew he was under the influence. But he had a great tolerance for alcohol. He promised to call back in the morning. Just hoped he'd remember.

We had spent about an hour on the project, but Red's girlfriend, Jen, was on her way over. Hot stuff she was, but I pretended not to notice. And then Rita arrived back. She had a takeaway steak sandwich waiting for me. You guys have all been in this position. I had bad acid indigestion from the curry, and I had to feign delight about stuffing down a steak sandwich. I put half of it in my pocket when she wasn't looking. And then we turned on Dancing with the Stars. There was fuck all dancing and very few stars but a lot of flesh. I fell asleep within minutes. I woke up in the middle of the night and crawled into bed. Rita was still awake. How can I put this delicately? Let's say she was more than interested. I think you know what I mean. I said I had a gastrointestinal problem. Well, it sounded better than saying I had a headache. That's a woman's excuse. She said it was probably the curry. How the fuck did she work that out?

The following morning, just after Red's girl had slipped out, Louie called me. Holy shit, did this guy ever sleep? Probably not. He said he had checked the police records and said that they had no record of Marie having called them. But he had some good news. He had found two guys named Eric Horsfall. Both of them lived in Inglewood, which was close to downtown Calgary. He provided me with a couple of addresses. This was going to be easy. Money for old rope, as they used to say.

Inglewood is old-time Calgary. It was probably a separate hamlet in the day. It was now an odd mix of bungalows and older red brick merchant buildings. I liked it. It had character. I promised Red I would buy him breakfast at one of the diners just off the main drag. He was up for it. I only had a cup of tea. My stomach was still not up to more. We decided which address we would go to first. The most likely candidate was living in a basement suite just a hundred yards from where we were.

As we left the diner, I noticed a poster on the wall. The Great Boudin, the Silent Illusionist, would be presenting over two nights at the Jubilee Auditorium in a couple of weeks and would also be doing a charity show at the Pumphouse Theatre. The latter was for aged survivors of COVID-19 or something like that. Bit of a contrast between the two establishments. The Jube, as it was known to locals, was a huge 2,000-seat auditorium that could easily cope with Covid restrictions. The Pumphouse was a slightly run-down theatre, albeit with considerable character. It was one of Calgary's first pumping stations by the river and was a historical site. The theatre largely catered to Community Theatre. It had suffered badly after the coronavirus hit and was hanging on by its fingernails, as was Community Theatre.

It was decent of Boudin to do a charity show. You could bet your boots Copperfield and the like would not and certainly not at the Pumphouse Theatre. Perhaps Boudin was the generous type. And so was Red. He paid the bill. I tore the poster off the wall and stuffed it in my pocket.

I wasn't too sure what we would say to Eric Horsfall when and if we found him. I could lecture him on making threats, but he could easily just tell us to fuck off. He lived in a bungalow off the main street. It looked cared for in a way that I didn't. We knocked on the door. A matronly, grey-haired woman answered. I tried to sound like a cop.

"Excuse me, madam, we are trying to track down Mr. Eric Horsfall," I said. "He has come into some money. A distant relative. We thought he should know." I swear I heard Red groan. He was never comfortable with bullshit.

"Well, you've come to the right place," she replied. "But here's not here now."

"When will he be back?" I said.

"He won't be back."

"Owes a bit of back rent, does he?"

"Mr. Horsfall was a very nice old man. Rented my basement suite for the last five years. It was sad to see what happened."

"Meaning?"

"He was admitted to hospital last week with advanced dementia, emphysema, and coronary heart disease. He died of the Covid virus a couple of days ago."

"How old was he?"

"He was certainly over 90. I think he'd stopped counting." Shit, he'd obviously stopped breathing. This was not our man.

"Well, we are sorry to have troubled you," I said. "Thanks for your help." I turned to leave.

"What about the inheritance?" she queried, as she followed me out of the door.

"It was only two hundred dollars, and it will be stuck in probate for a while. We'll contact the next of kin in due course," I replied.

That narrowed the field a bit. In fact, it narrowed it down completely. We only had one other name, and he lived at the other end of 10th Ave. I would have driven there, but Red did point out that my cardiologist had advised more exercise. Did I mention I had a heart attack six months ago? A mild one. Of course, we all say that. My father said the same thing. He lasted six months. So, we set off the 800 yards to the apartment. It was on the east end of 10th Ave, so I guessed it was probably over a store. I was right. It was over Deacons, a previously enjoyed furniture store. It was no longer presently enjoyed. Like many of the shops in the neighbourhood, it had closed down months before. There was a side entrance that led to several one-bedroom apartments. This was cheap accommodation. The stairs were dusty and unswept. There was graffiti on the walls. There was the smell of curry and stale piss wafting through the corridor. I suddenly felt another wave of acid reflux.

Apartment 1B was non-descript. The door seemed to have been forced at one time. We knocked. There was no reply. After a few seconds, the door at the end of the corridor opened. A Sikh gentleman stood there. That explained the curry.

"Can I help you, gentleman? I'm the landlord," he asked.

"We're looking for Mr. Horsfall," I replied.

"Investigations Unit, Canada Revenue Agency," added Red. That was brilliant. You only have to mention the Canada Revenue Agency, and sphincters usually tighten quickly.

"I haven't seen him, I'm afraid," he replied.

"When was the last time you saw him?"

"I've never met him. It was all done through the internet. He paid a deposit. I left the key in his letter slot."

"Isn't that a bit strange?" I said.

"Yes, it is, but I know he's been there."

"How?"

"I've heard him rooting around in his room. And besides, he picks up his post." He pointed to the row of letter boxes on the wall.

"There's something in there. Mind if I look?"

"Be my guest," he replied.

There was not much to see. A two-for-one suit sale from Moore's, a flyer from London Drugs, and a 50% off deal from a landscaping company. None of these had an address on them, but one did. It was from the Apex Ticketing Agency. It showed that the ticket for the upcoming Boudin concert had been processed. Didn't say which one, but this suggested that we had found our man.

"Well, I think we'll be back," I said to the landlord. I turned to leave but kept the Moore's flyer. I needed a new suit. You can only sandpaper the shiny arse of your suit so many times.

We wandered back to the diner. That knocked 5, 000 steps off my daily requirement. All we had to do was to find this guy. I mean, we could have set up a dusk till dawn surveillance, but there might be a better way.

"What do you think?" I said to Red.

"We could install a miniature video camera in there. Nobody would notice," he suggested.

So, there was a better way. The only problem was that we didn't have a video camera and it might be beyond our budget. And then Red came up with an even better idea.

"Why don't we just drop by and accidentally find the door open," said Red.

"Strange how some people forget to close their doors. We couldn't possibly think of breaking in." I winked at Red. He smiled.

"Of course, not boss," he answered.

I knew this would be easy for Red. He was an honest guy, but he had a bit of a history. He knew how to do all sorts of things, such as break-ins and hot-wiring cars. A misspent youth, I suppose. Never got caught but a few close shaves. So, we decided to go in there that night. If Horsfall was there, that would work. If not, we could still find out a bit more about him. After another coffee, we split. Red had to get his Covid vaccination. So did I, for that matter, but I claimed a religious exemption. Funny that. I'd always described myself as a born-again atheist.

One thing that is a consequence of a coronary is that you always like to nap. So, I went home with that in mind. It was when I walked in I knew that the shit was about to hit the fan. Rita looked to be in a mood.

"Everything OK, my love?" I said.

"I'm fine," she replied. It wasn't fine. She was holding a half-chewed steak sandwich in her hand.

"What do you call this?" I mean, there was no answer to that question. Well, not the obvious one.

"The dog found it in your jeans pocket this morning. She might as well finish it." She threw the meat at Nancy, our dog, who wolfed it down. Not the best idea.

Let me tell you about Nancy, our bulldog cross. Great disposition but a dodgy digestive system. You see, she tended to fart when she ate meat. The first time I went back to Rita's place, I thought it was Rita.

Anyway, I had to make amends for the steak. I had an idea. Changing the subject was the first step. Flattery was the second.

"You've been so helpful in the past, honey. Couldn't do my job without you," I said quietly. And she had been helpful in the past. She sat in her wheelchair one day doing surveillance for us. She begged people for money. Made more than we did that day.

"What do you want, Sidney?" At least she was being civil.

"Look baby, you know your brother works in that electronics store downtown. Any chance we could get a mini-surveillance system on spec," I said.

"If you ask really nicely," she replied.

"OK, I'll say please," I muttered. "And if he comes though, I'll say thank you."

"You're a real arsehole, Sidney," she replied. Back on track with the old girl. This was my Rita. She laughed and picked up the phone. She called her brother. We could have it the next day, but only for a week.

"Thanks, honey," I said. "Perhaps we can watch Dancing with the Stars again tonight. It was good last night." Oh, shit. I didn't mean to go that far. But you have to reward good behaviour. It worked. I kicked the dog out into the yard to fart some more, and we had a great night. We even held hands.

The next day, we woke to the sound of the doorbell ringing. It was Rita's brother Phil who told us to be careful with the camera system. He handed it to me. I put it on the kitchen table and then remembered that I'd left the dog out all night. Poor bugger. He'd slept on the doorstep. I knew how that felt.

I banged on the floor to wake Red up, but he'd been working on how we could unobtrusively install the video system. He was good at that sort of thing. I was fucking useless. I was still communicating with the world on my flip phone when I remembered to charge the battery. And I never listened to voice messages. If they wanted to get hold of me, they could call me back.

We had a quick coffee and decided on our plan of action for the day. It was too early to go back to Horsfall's apartment, so we decided to go down to the Pumphouse Theatre to check on Boudin's performance schedule. It should have been easy to get there, but there was a mass demonstration against the Covid lockdowns in downtown Calgary. None of them were wearing masks. I didn't have an opinion on masks, but I had been involved in a couple of cases where there had been a couple of bank robberies. Identification was difficult...no, it was impossible because the bad guys were wearing masks and so was everybody else. In my day, the cops would have been all over anyone walking into a bank in a mask. You could easily get shot. It was an accident waiting to happen.

4

INGLEWOOD

The Pumphouse Theatre is just off Bow Trail. It was a neat venue, albeit a little jaded, and awaiting some desperately needed improvements. The staff performed miracles to keep it running. An investment of a few million could have made it into the sort of arts venue that other cities would have been proud of. All I wanted to know was whether Horsfall had been in the office to book his ticket. He had. They remembered him quite well. A slightly built, brusque individual, but they probably wouldn't recognize him again. With a mask, aviator shades, and a ball cap, he could have been anybody. He could have been the invisible man. But they remembered him. He seemed to be a bit different from their usual clientele. And why had they remembered him? He made some unusual comments. He wanted a specific seat in the theatre, but he also wanted to know if the full theatre was being used. Let me explain. If a smaller crowd was expected, the auditorium would be curtained off to a smaller configuration. A bigger crowd would necessitate opening up the full theatre. Since booking had only just begun, they couldn't tell him one way or the other. Besides, it was usually first come first served. He could sit where he wanted so long as he was six feet away from the next person. And that was that. They didn't see him again.

Red and I walked back into town. I was getting an odd feeling about this case. A bit like eating bad shellfish and knowing that you are going to throw up...eventually. You keep telling yourself you'll be

OK but ......And that's what I felt about this case. There was something wrong here, but I couldn't say what. I just knew.

On the way back into town, I got a couple of calls. One from the wife of a cabinet minister who thought her husband was going away to Canmore with his secretary. Do they still call them secretaries these days? Anyway, I still do. She wanted us to follow him and report back. Follow him. How? In Walid's van. I told her to check his toiletry bag and if he had bought a couple of new smellies, that would answer the question. And then, right on cue, Walid phoned. He wanted the latest payment for his van. I told him there was a cheque in the post. I asked Red to find out what 'fuck off' was in Lebanese.

Once in the downtown area, Red and I went our separate ways. I took the bus home, but Red had a more interesting assignment. He'd done a few stints as a movie extra. You guessed it. In Westerns. But this hunk could act. He had the look. That certain something. He could have been the Marlborough Man in another era. This time he was auditioning for a part in an advertisement. He was probably wasting his time. Let's face it. How many indigenous people do you see in adverts? I'll tell you. None. But nothing ventured, nothing gained, as they say.

I went home and picked up my old reliable. It was a Honda Civic, 15 years old, leaked oil but got me around. My thirty-year-old truck was not reliable. It had been in for repairs for a couple of months. It was an expensive bill. I'd get around to paying for the repairs when I had the money.

It was time to check out Boudin's warehouse. I had nothing better to do. It was situated by the Bonnybrook Waste Disposal Plant. Hardly quiet and certainly not free of odours. The warehouse was tucked away on the edge of an industrial estate. It was easy to find, though there was no signage outside the warehouse at all. Just a few bits and pieces from old illusions were dumped outside. A BMW with the license plate MRMAGIC sat outside.

I was about to get out of the car when a side door opened and Marie stepped outside. She didn't see me. I was parked across the road. She was followed by a well-built, middle-aged man. They hugged, but as they did so, she noticed me and separated from him rather quickly. He turned and left by the side of the building. She waved me over.

"A friend?" I queried, but it was none of my business.

"My new effects man. You know theatre people. Always hugging." Hmm...a bit of a guilty conscience there, I thought. She didn't have to say that.

"I didn't notice," I replied.

"What can I do for you? I'm sorry Pierre is away for a few days."

"Nothing I can think of. I was just passing and thought you might like to know that we found Horsfall."

"You did. What did he have to say for himself?"

"He said nothing because we didn't actually meet him. Found out where he lived, though."

"Good to see you're making progress," she replied.

"We'll have a lot more information after the next couple of days. We're setting up a video camera outside his apartment."

"Is that necessary?" She looked uncomfortable about this turn of events.

"Maybe not. But I would certainly want to know who we're dealing with."

"Whereabouts is he?"

"Here's the address. I've scribbled it out on this slip of paper." I passed it to her. But don't think about doing anything silly," I said.

"Of course not," she replied. "I'm no hero. I'm paying you big bucks to look after this."

"Anyway, I was just passing. I'll stay in touch."

"Oh, I forgot to mention," she said. "I'll send over a couple of tickets for you and a date for the Pumphouse show."

"I'll take Red," I said. Hoped she didn't get the wrong idea.

I bade my farewell and walked back to my car. I had left her with the address, and I had also left a few spots of oil on the road. Didn't know I still had any oil left. There were a few questions I didn't ask about her new effects man. I never asked about the BMW. It had to be Boudin's.

A few hours later, I met up with Red at the diner in Inglewood. He looked pleased with himself. And he should have been pleased. He got the part in the TV advert. Society had taken a major step forward using an indigenous actor. But he was cast as the 'before man' in a shaving advert. OK, half a step forward. Better than nothing. But unquestionably, things would have to change.

We decided to go up to the apartment after ten that night. Horsfall would likely be there, but if not, we could install the camera without being disturbed. After several coffees, we strolled up to the Deacons store and made our way up the stairs. It was all quiet except for music coming from Horsfall's room. Light seeped from under the door. Damm. He must be in. Red knocked several times over the next couple of minutes, but not loud enough to alarm any of the other residents. We didn't really have a cover story if he answered, but then again, we never thought he'd be there. Just a gut feeling, and it proved correct. There was nobody in. We decided to poke around inside. A credit card doesn't always work to open a door, but it did in this case. The door opened rather easily. We stepped inside. There was not much to see. The radio was tuned to pop classics of the seventies. Didn't mean a thing, I suppose, but we could probably rule out anybody under the age of 30.

There was a case beside the bed. It was open. This guy knew how to pack. I just threw things in. His clothes were neatly arranged, and a few were neatly placed on the bed. This guy was tidy. He had either carefully remade his bed, or he hadn't slept in it.

I didn't notice this, but Red did. There was a tag on the case from Holloway's Exclusive Holidays. Not a cheap deal and, as described, it was very exclusive. It was for a holiday in China. Not what you would expect in a cheap one-bedroom apartment. This fella had expensive tastes.

There was no doubt that this guy had written the threatening letter. There was the pad from which the original note had clearly been torn. More incriminating was the fountain pen that sat on the desk and had been used in the letter, or so it seemed. Red had never seen a fountain pen before. You rarely see them at all these days.

If there had been any doubt, there was a book sitting on the bedside table. It told the whole story. It was entitled 'How to Get Away with Murder.' I mean, who the fuck writes this sort of crap? Most murderers know how to do it. They don't need any help.

There was nothing else of note. But there was more than enough evidence here to raise quite a few concerns. Oh, I forgot. There was something else. I found a lady's razor and a stick of female deodorant in the bathroom. Probably left there by a previous resident. If not, we might be looking for a homicidal cross-dresser. The video surveillance might be quite telling.

It did not take long to install the video camera. We placed it just over and inside the door. Even if you looked directly at it, you weren't likely to see it. And the picture was very clear. The only problem was that we had to record it on a computer that was situated nearby. We couldn't sit on the stairs and monitor it, but we came up with a solution that worked. We could monitor it from Walid's van. All it needed was someone in the van. It had to be parked nearby. Rita was always up for this sort of thing. If I told her it could break the case, she'd begin to salivate. She agreed to do it. I said I would order the last three seasons of Dancing with the Stars as a reward. But I didn't say I would help her watch them.

Once we had set the camera. We left as quickly as possible. But as we walked into the corridor, the next apartment door opened and a grizzled, toothless face emerged.

"Can you turn that fucking music down?" he barked. "I'm on the early shift tomorrow."

"Not a problem," said Red. But it was. The door had just clicked shut.

This needed some quick thinking. That was probably not coming from me.

"Shit, I've just locked myself out," said Red.

"You dickhead," I replied. "How are we going to get back in?"

"Not a problem", said the man. "I'll just get the landlord." He took a step forward.

And now the quick thinking.

"Not a problem, dude. I've got the spare key in my car," urged Red.

Holy fuck. That was quick thinking.

"Yeah, I'll be back in a minute," Red said. We both hurried down the stairs. We had not gone five yards when Red turned back.

"Where the fuck are you going?" I said.

"I'll go back and turn the radio off. What if he keeps complaining?"

"What if Horsfall comes back and discovers the radio has been turned off?" He'll be suspicious.

"Hmm... I didn't think about that." And that was Red all over. When he thought, he could be really quick thinking. When he didn't, he could be as thick as...Nah, I'm not going to finish that. Red was my buddy. That's all I have to say.

Eric Horsfall was out there somewhere, but it was a few days before we got an inkling he even existed. It had taken three days for him to emerge. Even Rita was getting bored and then, on the third day, there was some action. Not much. A figure emerged through the door, but here was the odd part of it. It was impossible to see who it was. He, and I am assuming it was a 'he', entered the apartment in the middle of the night. He wore a mask, a hoodie, and shades. It was impossible to see his face. The figure disappeared into the bathroom for about 5 minutes. He may have been taking a dump. He may have been using the lady's razor. Then he turned off the radio and left. I mean, it just made little sense. This guy must have been living somewhere else. Who was this character? Was it even Eric Horsfall? Perhaps Horsfall was on to the fact that we were watching him. Was someone simply trying to give the impression that somebody lived there? Perhaps it was a burglar. That might explain his attempt to hide his identity. But there was nothing to steal. There were a thousand explanations, but none that was convincing.

And then a couple of days later, he appeared again. This time, he checked the room as if he was looking for something. And he found it. He put a piece of tape over the camera. How the hell did he spot that? That was it as far as the camera went. We had to have it back to Phil the next day. I hoped it was not damaged.

That night, we took one last trip up the stairs at Deacons. I suppose it was inevitable that we would bump into the guy from the other night. He seemed in a much better mood.

"Thanks for turning the radio off. It was pissing me off," he said.

"Least we could do," said Red.

I turned towards the apartment door. There was a note stapled to it. 'Turn that fucking radio down.' It could have been him who had broken in, I suppose. We hadn't thought about it but nah, he didn't look as if he had a credit card.

Once he had disappeared, Red eased the door open. The camera was covered with tape, but it was not damaged. A bit of alcohol on the lens and it would be as good as new. We left as quickly as we had arrived. But I did have one idea. I knocked on the landlord's door. When he opened it, I reminded him we were from the Canada Revenue Agency. Did he have Mr. Horsfall's number? He ventured back into his apartment and returned with a sheet of paper. He did have a cell phone number. Progress at last.

That progress did not last long. We called the number, but it was one of those phones you buy at a convenience store. We would have no answers there.

Rita drove Walid's van back home, and I followed in the Civic. When we arrived home, there was a packet from Amazon on the doorstep. Rita opened it. It was the last 5 seasons of Dancing with the Stars. Damn, I thought I had only ordered three seasons. I tried to look interested that night, but all I could think of was who the fuck was this Horsfall guy and what was his game.

5

THEY CALL ME RED

I had three days before Red got back. He'd gone up to Canmore with his chick for a bit of rest and recreation. Course, we know what the recreation was. I would have done the same at his age. I'd do the same right now, but the women don't exactly have me on speed dial.

Since I have a few moments, let me tell you a bit more about Red. It sounds like bullshit if I say he was the son I never had, but it's true. Well, it wouldn't be entirely accurate. I had a son who died when he was two weeks old. Despite having three wives, there were to be no other children and precious little sex, for that matter.

I met Red when he was giving testimony in a court case. His brother was up on charges. I was on the prosecution side for the police. I think his brother got off, but I met Red outside. He seemed an intelligent young man. He impressed me with his dignity. And he was imposing. He reminded me of what Atticus Finch might have been if he had been indigenous. Then again, he was wearing his Pioneer Wrestling t-shirt and frayed jeans. Softly spoken, his grandpa glasses harkened back to the sixties. Put him in a three-piece suit and he would look like a defence lawyer. I was intrigued by this guy. I told him I would buy him a coffee and a sandwich. I think he needed one. He was to tell me his story over the next few weeks.

Red had come from a broken background all too familiar these days. His father had disappeared when he was two years old, and his mother died of tuberculosis when he was 6. His grandmother raised him and she did a damn fine job. I know he got involved in drugs and alcohol for a time, but granny kicked his ass and that was that. He somehow kept his education going and though he did not immediately pass Grade 12, he took an online course and eventually passed. It was then he decided to come to Calgary, and he started to train as a wrestler. He wasn't bad. I went to Pioneer Wrestling years back and I think I remember seeing him. Played the heel, which was so much out of character, but he did it so well. The audience hated him. If only they had known.

Look, I know you're thinking that professional wrestling is unsophisticated and why do I watch it? It might be low brow but some of my best mates were wrestlers. To me, professional wrestling is nothing more than Dancing with the Stars with a bit more violence and better acting than I see on daytime TV.

Anyway, back to Red. He lived in a one-room apartment and when I met him he was wondering what he could do. He thought about trying to go to college but lacked the funds. I told him that Indian Affairs might help him, and they did. He eventually enrolled in a course called Criminal Justice for two years. But he was still financially challenged. I wanted to help him out and offered him a room in my house in Beddington. That's in the northwest segment of the city. My third wife had already left, but I had been allowed to keep the house for a time. Yes, fellas, it happens sometimes. She made her fortune the old-fashioned way. She married into it. Her boss was one of the city's top lawyers. He was 20 years older than her, but he was loaded. Bugger all personality, but she could live the life of the rich and famous out in Bearspaw, and sex once a month would only be a small price to play.

Red did some odd jobs to keep himself going. Convenience stores, that sort of thing. But he couldn't pay me a cent. He helped in other ways. Cooking. Great cook, especially with Indigenous dishes and he was especially useful doing any heavy work around the house. By that time, I'd messed my back up. But he still needed money for textbooks, and he'd just got a girlfriend. Tough to take out a date with no money.

I know you'll think I'm a soft touch, but.... Look, one night I saw an opportunity to help. We were doing a big drug bust just off 17th Ave SW. Idiots kept a shitload of money in their house and I mean a shitload. When I picked it up, I took it down to the station, but on the way home I realized that there was a package of money still on the floor of the car. I'd have to return it, or did I? Those crooks had no idea how much was there. The money sat there for two weeks, and nothing was said. I thought I'd be a latter-day Robin Hood. I gave three grand to Red and the rest to charity. Told Red I'd won it at the casino. He didn't want to take it, but I told him I had a deal for him. Once graduated, he could come and work with me. I was thinking of setting up a detective agency. He agreed. He had funds to keep him going, and I had enough left for a six-pack and a pack of cigs. Not too proud of this and I'd be obliged if you kept it to yourself.

Red worked his tail off. He left me far behind when it came to academic affairs. He would read anything: philosophy, science, history, political affairs. You get the idea. Most of the time, I didn't have a fucking clue. One day, over breakfast, he was deep into the pages of a book. He put it down and said.

"Voltaire... what do you think?"

I was typically the sort of guy who could bullshit himself out of anything, but Voltaire had me stumped. And then I realized.

"Probably get a lot of mileage from that," I said. He looked at me oddly.

"Well, yes, you would. Voltaire's writings are important in contemporary thought," he replied.

Shit, I thought the Voltaire was the latest Chevrolet battery-driven car. He didn't notice, and then his cell phone rang.

It was shortly after that, I met Debra. After three failed marriages, I should have known better. She was the sort of gal who would throw herself at men. She usually missed. Not with me. What was it? The need for affection. Or did I want a regular screw? As it turned out, I got neither. And she drank too much. Not sure how she got her hooks into Red. I know she could be a real sexy beast when she wanted to. And she knew all the buttons to push. I know she had found my buttons all too easily. Anyway, enough of that. As I explained earlier Red, and I soon buried the hatchet and I moved on to live with Rita. And that's where we are today.

Oh, I should add that Red graduated and lived up to his agreement to work for Lou Diamond. I knew he would move on eventually, but I could afford to pay him a decent wage. Did I mention I sold my house and though my ex got half the proceeds? I made that money go a long way. That takes us up to today. Has he changed? Not a bit. He still reads Voltaire. I mean, who the fuck is this guy?

I've told you about Red, and so I better tell you about myself. Not everything about me. I do have a few warts. I have already told you a few. I was originally from the UK. The industrial north. We were poor, though I never realized it. Never thought about it. I just thought I was happy, and I suppose I was. I had a twin brother. People ask if we are identical. Not even close. He's got money, I'd say. He got tapped on the shoulder by the queen a few years back. No, I was never rich. Never famous. As a kid, I was always generous and always shared my candies. I suppose I still am generous. Let's face it, people are usually rich because they inherit it, or they give fuck all away. I can't tick off any of those boxes.

I came to Calgary 40 years ago just after I left university. But I still have the accent to prove it. Well, not exactly. People tell me I have a mid-Atlantic accent. Perhaps they think I come from Iceland. I said that I left university. What I didn't say was that I never completed university. I had signed up to do engineering, but it wasn't for me. There were too many birds, too many parties. I'll tell you a secret. I did a few drugs. Not the really hard stuff. First time I've admitted that. Shit, everybody does drugs these days. Well, everybody but me....... OK, not often. Booze got me for a time. But that was easy to overcome.

When I arrived, Canadian beer was piss-poor. Today I'd say it was piss great. Times change.

I managed to get a few jobs related to engineering, but I always had an inkling to join the police. It didn't exactly run in the family, though my dad worked as a security guard. So did my mother, for that matter. It must have been in our genes. I first got married when I was 22. It was lust at first sight. Great legs. Not much of a basis for a long-term marriage, and so it proved. Those long legs walked away after two years. Then I joined the cops. There were perks. I got to wear a uniform for the first time. Most people said that it was the first time they had seen me looking smart. They had a point. I took the job seriously, and I was good at it. I was a friendly cop. Always ready with a joke, always ready to diffuse a situation. I never saw much violence. Most of the time, if you were friendly, it wasn't a problem. The bad guys usually didn't want to fight either. I did get a commendation once. I talked down this guy who had climbed 60 feet up a radio tower. People rarely do that unless they are suicidal. And he was suicidal. I put him in my car and drove him to the psychiatric emergency at the hospital. They admitted him and I was proud of what I had achieved. Three days later, after a long weekend, I received a phone call from the hospital telling me he had hanged himself. They discharged him after 48 hours. Sometimes you can only do what you can do.

When I left the police, under the unfortunate circumstances that I described, I set up Lou Diamond investigations. You might wonder where I got the name from. Lou was a secondhand car dealer who bilked me out of a few grand years before. You know the deal. Wind the mileage down 60,000 km. For some reason, the name resonated with me perhaps because I was still angry with the prick after 30 years, so I decided to use it.

You might wonder where my financing came from. Remember that I had just sold my house. And I had a lot of contacts both inside and outside the law. One of the first big contracts was with the Worker's Compensation Board. You know the situation. I've got a bad back, and

I haven't been able to work for years. Most of their special services division were ex-cops, so I had a bit of a leg up there. One of my first assignments demonstrated to me how smart Red was. We were asked to surveil this fella down in Lethbridge. We did have an old camera at the time; it was bulky and looked like a TV camera. Still, it worked. This guy said that he was in constant pain and had to use a special orthopedic seat. This was not at all evident at the local hockey rink. He sat on the bench with his teammates. Nothing orthopedic there. It looked just like any other wooden bench. The problem was, how could we videotape this man without him guessing that he was under surveillance? I had no idea, but Red did. He went across the ice and told the guy he was doing a documentary for television on old-timers' hockey. Would they mind if we filmed them? Mind? Our guy took it all very seriously and probably had more assists in the first 10 minutes than he had had in years. This made our reputation. It made him ill. He had to pay back thousands. We got a lot more work.

Then came COVID-19. Sure, we still had a bit of work to do. Most of it was from folks who'd had a dream about some ex-girlfriend or boyfriend. Could we find them? Usually not a problem. All in a day's work. The only problem was that once we found them and sent a picture, we never heard from them again. It's funny. You always dream of ex-flames as they were. Years later, they have often put on sixty pounds or gone bald......usually but not always the men.

The bottom line was that we were having fun despite Covid. We had kept our heads above water and developed a bit of reputation... some of it positive.

6

My name is Horgan

Just before Red got back, I dropped in to see a friend of mine who owned a magic shop in the Northeast part of the city. The reason was twofold. It was Red's birthday coming up, and I thought I might buy him a book about magic. Remember, I said he had an interest in magic and illusions. I asked the proprietor for a good idea. He pointed out a book called Chung Ling Soo: The Marvelous Chinese Conjuror. Meant nothing to me. So long as it wasn't in Chinese, it would do the trick. Now I'm not telling you this to prove what a nice guy I am. This book had some relevance to our case, though. I didn't realize it at the time, but I hope you eventually will.

As I left, I asked the proprietor what he thought of Boudin. He wasn't exactly effusive. Said he was alright, but his act was wearing thin. He wouldn't be attending any of the shows in Calgary, though he was selling some tickets for the charity show. He told me that Boudin had added a new illusion to his show. I asked him about it and how it was done. He told me to bugger off. Couldn't give away secrets. He was a member of the Magic Circle, and he wanted it to stay that way.

I had arranged to meet Red in the pub next door. As I said, Red did not drink except on very rare occasions. Neither did I, most of the time. I tried to be a good boy. When he ordered, he would buy me a beer. Usually non-alcoholic or light, but not on this occasion. There it was, waiting for me. A cold pint of dark craft brew. Oh well, it wouldn't do me any harm if I sipped it slowly.

I gave Red the book. I knew it was his birthday next week, but so what? I'd probably forget otherwise. He seemed genuinely pleased. Said he'd heard of this character. William Robinson. Who the fuck was that? I thought it was about Chung Ling Soo. He promised to have it read that week. It was 500 pages long. He was out on a surveillance job that week, so he had plenty of time and he was a fast reader. And then he told me he had thought of buying me a book. When I asked him what, he said that there was a new biography of Voltaire that had just come out. Now he was taking the piss. At least, I hoped he was.

We talked for a few minutes about the investigation so far. Not much had been achieved, but Marie still wanted us to keep going. At the going rate of pay, we would be happy to oblige. And then he remembered there was a TV interview on that day with Boudin. It was on Artsvest, an art and culture program with the rotund and jocular host, Seamus Doyle. He was East Indian. I know it didn't sound like it. Perhaps his mother was Irish. They say that the Irish love potatoes. Seamus certainly did. He was pounds overweight and would perspire badly under the studio lights. He was always dabbing his brow. But he was a genuine character and beloved in the arts community.

Now you might ask how the hell we were going to watch an arts program in a pub. One thing you might have forgotten was that social distancing and all that crap had decimated pubs. The lunchtime crowd had all but disappeared. In this pub, it had completely disappeared. We were the only ones there. Nobody was watching sports. We could have watched anything.

I'll give Seamus his due. He made Boudin seem like the second coming. That's how he treated all his guests. I think most of the information came from a press release. That being said, Seamus could always ask the tough questions. Boudin was pretty much as I'd expected. He could have been the prototypical Parisian in a comedy sketch. He had short dark hair parted in the middle and a thin handlebar mustache. That meant that it curled up a bit at the ends. A pince-nez dangled from his jacket pocket. There was not one white hair. I wondered what hair dye he was using. I could use some of that. It was a dated look but said in 3D, I'm a Frenchman. Red thought he looked like an anorexic cross between Inspector Clouseau and Poirot. And he had one other thing. An accent that was so strong it was almost incomprehensible. He had obviously been taking lessons from Marie. Perhaps they had been practicing together.

Seamus could usually glean something from nothing. And this was nothing. Boudin answered monosyllabically. Not bad for someone who was supposed to be silent. What we found out came in the first five minutes. He was born in Paris and baptized at Notre Dame. Now that was ladling it on a bit too much. He claimed he was an advisor for the Surete in France. Odd that. The Surete was renamed in 1964 before he was born. All sounded like a load of bollocks to me. And then he mentioned that he studied the techniques of the famous Chinese Illusionist Wen Fu. I checked that out, and this guy existed at least according to Wikipedia. Boudin said he was fluent in Chinese. Fuck, he wasn't even fluent in English.

To be fair, Boudin let his fingers do the talking. He performed a couple of card tricks and the billiard ball illusion. That's where one billiard ball becomes 5 in his hand. And that was impressive. Red even told me how he did it, but you'd have to practice for years to do it. And you certainly couldn't do it after a couple of craft beers.

Seamus was under the illusion that he could get 30 minutes of material from Boudin. But the interview pretty much died after 15 minutes. I told you Seamus tended to sweat. He was dabbing his face every few seconds. I knew he was desperate when he asked if magic might help society with the COVID-19 pandemic. Boudin shrugged his shoulders and then pointed out that he would be revealing an illusion first performed in the Wen Fu Dynasty 2,000 years ago. If you ask me, this guy was more Wanking than Peking. Seamus dabbed his face again and thanked Boudin for the interview. Boudin uttered something incomprehensible in what was supposed to be Chinese. Frankly, it could have been curried beef, number 49 on the menu.

I don't think I expected much, and I was right. Red was quite impressed with Boudin's prestidigitation skills but didn't think the interview would do much for ticket sales. Since he was back in town, we decided it might be a good idea to pop over to the warehouse and have a chat with Boudin if he was there. I mean, someone had to tell him about the threats. It was the only idea we had. We had yet to finger the elusive Eric Horsfall. We were definitely treading water in this case.

It only took us 10 minutes to get up to Bonnybrook. The area was quite deserted. Many of the small companies around there had long since shut down. When we arrived at the warehouse, there was a motorbike parked outside. Not quite something Boudin would use, but we knocked on the door, anyway. The door was opened by somebody who looked quite familiar. It was Mr. Huggy from a few days before.

"Sorry to disturb you," I said. "We were looking for Monsieur Boudin."

"Not here," he replied firmly.

"He arranged to meet us here to show us around the warehouse." Sometimes I didn't even know I was lying.

"And you are?"

"Sidney Arbuckle, private eye, and my assistant Red."

"I've heard Marie talk about you, so it can't do any harm," he said. He ushered us into the front office.

"I don't believe we've met before," I said.

"No, I don't think so. My name is Stephen Horgan. I'm the chief engineering construction advisor." He was informally dressed in jeans and a sweater. The sweater stood out. It was quite an unusual shade of green. You rarely see green these days. Chief Engineering construction advisor. Nice moniker for someone who could probably only use a screwdriver and a tube of instant glue.

"Mind if we sit down for a moment?" I said. He nodded.

"What can I do for you?" he replied.

"You could almost say this is a social visit. We were just passing."

"Well, good to meet you. Would you like a coffee?"

Good idea, I thought. It could extend the conversation for a while. I nodded.

"How would you like it? Black or......black. Afraid we've run out of cream and sugar."

"No problem", said Red. It was for me. I have chronic acid indigestion. I like it diluted a bit.

As he prepared the coffee, we both scanned the office. There was a desk, a bookcase, and several pieces of equipment that were being stored. There was a wicker trunk in the middle of the floor. The sort of thing that usually stored costumes. People could sit on that. A few posters lined the wall. Apart from that, there was little to see. We both noticed a button on the wall that would allow people to come in from outside.

"Gentleman. Your coffee." He served them in Boudin-labeled mugs.

I decided to get right to the point.

"We've been checking up on this guy, Eric Horsfall. I don't suppose you know him."

"Actually, I do," he said. "I took over from him when he was fired."

"Fired?"

"He was a strange character. He was very skilled but ...... well, he was a bit odd."

"In what way?" said Red.

"He seemed bitter.......angry, resentful. He felt he was not given enough credit. Thought Boudin had pla...plag......"

"Plagiarized", I said. Made me feel superior for a moment. Why couldn't folks remember this word?

"That's right. Plagiarized. You've seen it before, I'm sure. The disenchanted employee."

"Did you know he had made some threats to Boudin?" I replied.

"Good heavens. Who could have imagined? I know he seems obsessed with getting some sort of retribution. I knew he had a bit of a violent streak. Apparently, he had been done for assault a few years back. Slapped his wife around. Said he was misunderstood most of his life.".

Who could have imagined? Everybody could, I thought to myself. This guy didn't have much of an imagination.

"Do you know where he is now?"

"As a matter of fact, I do. I had to drop some of his tools off when he left. He's got an apartment in Inglewood. Just above the old Deacons store."

"Was he in when you visited with him?"

"He was just going out when I got there. He didn't say much. I haven't seen him since."

"Do you know why he was fired?"

"Look, I think you could guess. He was a troublemaker. He even threatened me once."

"I think we get the idea," I said.

At this point, I thought it might be worthwhile to look at the warehouse and Horgan agreed to show us around. Before we did, Red said that he had been drinking too much coffee and could he use the bathroom. I'll let you into a secret. It was nothing urgent. But there was a method to this. You would be surprised at what some people store in their bathrooms. Sometimes nothing more than a toilet brush, sometimes more. There was nothing too significant here. Some old posters and a couple of books, 'The Annals of Magic' and 'How to Make People Disappear.' In Eric Horsfall's bathroom, that would have been suspicious. Perhaps it was suspicious here.

There was no doubt about it. The warehouse was a significant fire hazard. The place was crammed with what I guessed were parts of illusions and other magic paraphernalia. There was also a costume section. Now that was interesting. There was an almost exact replica of the Chinese costume depicted on the Chung Ling Soo book cover. There was also a large furnace. When I asked Horgan about it, he said that they didn't like to throw stuff away. There was always the chance that competitors would rummage through it. Trade secrets and all that. I couldn't imagine anyone wandering through Bonnybrook on the off chance that something would be thrown out from this place.

After ten minutes, we had seen everything, or at least everything, he was prepared to show us. We left and drove home. Red turned to me and said, "Something smells around here."'. He was not referring to me or the Bonnybrook Sewerage Plant. Red always had a nose for trouble.

When we got back home, there was a message waiting for me. Louie, remember my police contact, had called. Rita said that I should call him immediately on his cell phone. Now, what could this be about? Well, he had a lot of news. Nothing about Horsfall but plenty about Boudin and his wife. Pierre was not French. Imagine my shock. Boudin's real name was Doug Horton. He was born in Medicine Hat. Perhaps he was born on the left bank of.........the South Saskatchewan River. He had never traveled to China. How the fuck had Louie found that out? This guy's exposure to Chinese culture might have been limited to the Imperial Palace restaurant in Calgary. And then there was Marie. Not her real name. She was born in Red Deer. Not too much information about Marie or Doreen Morrisey, her real name. She had a minor criminal record. Shoplifting at Walmart when she was 14. I thought we all did that. Well, I did, but I was never caught. When she married Horton, she was working as a car detailer in Airdrie. That was just north of Calgary.

I was hardly surprised by this information. We are all guilty of telling fibs. But this was a bit more than embroidering your resume. Still, I suppose that's show business. I was still put off by Doreen's airs and graces. Who the fuck did she think she was? My mother had a term for these people. All fur coat and no knickers.

Of course, this news was hardly surprising, but certainly showed that the Boudins were guilty of lying. Not a good sign.

Two hours later, Louie called back. There had been sightings of Eric Horsfall. Sadly, one was in the morgue. We already knew that but the other, and hopefully our Eric had been seen around town. Just not by us. Louie said he would keep in touch. I didn't argue, but this was going to cost me far more than a six-pack.

7
ANOTHER MESSAGE

The trail was growing cold as far as Eric was concerned. And then Marie (so what if she was born Doreen Morrisey) called. She had some depressing news. She had received another message in the post. This time, the author demanded money. Pay up and I'll go away. The problem is that these people rarely go away, no matter what you pay them. She was understandably upset. I asked to meet with her again. In doing so, I accidentally called her Doreen. There was a brief pause. When she replied, her accent had completely disappeared. She suggested we might meet at the Ranchmen's Club. Shit, they wouldn't let me in there. That was a pretty exclusive place. It would certainly exclude someone from my questionable class. It had to be on my terms. I suggested my favourite biker bar. Great to keep the other person off balance. Besides, there were probably just as many crooks in the Ranchmen's Club as there were in Bernie's Bar. It's just that most of them had never been charged.

I'm not sure Bernie had intended that his bar would become home to the biking fraternity. It just sort of happened. Now you might think that an ex-cop in a biker bar was a bad idea. Not so. Sure, I'd put a few of them away, but I was always fair and most of them respected that. Besides, Rita used to work there behind the bar. She knew a few of these guys, not that she was a biker chick or anything like that. At least, she told me she hadn't been.

I arrived early and waited for Marie to arrive. When she did, she was still wearing a designer mask, but what a change. A denim shirt, jeans, and leather jacket didn't exactly make her a biker chick, but it didn't prompt any stares. When she ordered a gin and tonic, a few heads turned. I ordered a hot chocolate with a liberal shot of Jim Beam.

She spoke with a normal accent. She didn't say why. I obviously knew, and she knew I knew. After a few niceties, she got down to business.

"Mr. Arbuckle, as I told you on the phone, I received another message."

"Do you have it with you?" I said.

She nodded and pulled it out of her denim purse. Nice touch that. Nothing Gucci about that purse. It was handwritten on the same paper as the other messages. It was a bit rambling but, in brief, demanded ten thousand dollars in cash. The note demanded that the money be put in an envelope and placed on the southbound LRT train that left City Hall Station at exactly 10.43 PM that night. Just a minute, that was two days ago.

The money was to be placed down the side of the front seat of the front carriage. Failure to do this would have incalculable consequences, it said. This sounded like bullshit to me. This was extortion. I told her she should call the police.

"I'm afraid it's too late," she said.

"Too late. Holy shit, you didn't pay this, did you?'

"I tried, but we fucked it up."

"What do you mean, you fucked it up?"

"I put it on the wrong train. There had been a points failure on 7th Avenue, and we put it on the N.E train, which came by at 10.43. I had Steve Horgan waiting at the Stampede Station in the south. I had to call him and tell him to get his arse over to Saddletowne at the end of the northeast line."

"And did he?"

"Oh, he got the money back, but then I got a phone call."

"From Horsfall, I imagine."

"It was very unpleasant. He was furious. Said that we had double-crossed him. And that would be his final warning. I tried to reason with him. It didn't help."

"Did Horgan see who got on at Stampede Station?"

"Fuck. There was ten grand sitting on the wrong train. He had to get off his arse and get after it fast."

Funny how Mademoiselle's Parisian language had deteriorated into Anglo-Saxon expletives.

"Did he call you on your cell phone?" She nodded.

"Let me have a look at your phone," I said.

"It's the most recent call." She passed it to me. It was a number I had seen before. It was the throwaway cell that Horsfall had used before. That would not help, but I did try to call it. Not surprisingly, there was no answer.

"Oh, I forgot to mention," she said. "He knows all about you."

"He does?"

"He told me to get those wankers off the case. Don't waste your money on those clumsy dickheads or something like that."

"Must have been talking about somebody else. We're not clumsy," I said. She smiled. The first time my humour had any impact.

I wondered how we could have screwed up. It was a cardinal rule. Never let them know you're on the case.

"How did he find out, I wonder?" I said.

"I certainly never mentioned who you were."

"So, do you intend to take us dickheads off the case?"

"No way. I want you to be on his trail. This man is unhinged.".

I mean, how could I refuse? The Boudins seemed to have a spare ten grand. I had plenty of spare time.

"O.K. What do you want us to do?"

"See if you could find him. If you can't at least be at our performances next week. We need some security."

"When exactly are the performances?" I said.

"Wednesday at the Jubilee and Saturday at the Pumphouse."

"I'll put my best men on this," I replied.

"I think I owe you more in the way of payment. This should help." She passed me a cheque. I didn't look at it. I passed it on to Red later that day.

Marie knocked back her gin and tonic and jumped into her BMW outside. Probably leased. So was her drink. That would be charged to my expenses.

When I said that I would put my best men on the job, I wasn't being entirely honest. I knew that Red and I would be out of town the following day. We had been asked to find an illegal elk velvet processing plant near Rocky Mountain House. Big demand for this from China. In case you didn't know, elk velvet is used to put a bit more permanence to a man's passion. You know what I mean. I tried it myself when I met Rita. I didn't know whether to swallow it or rub it on. Didn't do much for me, either way. Anyway, we knew who the guys were. They were poachers. We just had to find the processing plant.

This left me with a bit of a problem. I didn't have a best man for the job. But I had the best woman. Rita had done this before. She was observant. No one would imagine she was doing surveillance. She would sit in her wheelchair at the side of the auditorium and watch. As I mentioned previously, she didn't actually need the wheelchair. She had discarded it years before, but it got her in the front row of the theatre.

We made no further progress on the Horsfall case that week. We kept a log of our efforts, though. Marie would need evidence that we had done something. We set out for Rocky Mountain House the night before Rita began surveillance at the theatre. Our instructions to Rita were to look for anything out of the ordinary. If there was nothing. Well, just enjoy the show and don't forget to pick up a program.

The next day, I called Marie to see if there had been any further developments. Nothing. I told her that our best associate would be at the Jube. I didn't tell her we thought Horsfall, if he showed up at all, would come to the Saturday show at the Pumphouse Theatre. Much less in the way of security there. She let me know that Boudin still did not know of the threats. Too sensitive. All very odd.

We found the processing plant with little effort. A bit of an exaggeration. It was in this guy's garage in Red Deer, a fair bit away from where we had been told. So, it was not a top-end operation. Just a couple of fellas who'd lost their jobs because of Covid and were trying to make a few dollars. I couldn't blame them. I might have done the same.

On the way back, Rita called. It had been an interesting night. She missed the start of the show because the taxi dropped her off at Jubilations Theatre. Jubilations was a theatre venue, all right. Just the wrong one. It was a somewhat low-brow venue that had put on fun shows and dinner theatre for an economic price for several years. And then came Covid. The economic price of social distancing was just not economic anymore. Somehow, they had survived despite the odds. Rita quickly realized she must have fucked up. Fortunately, the Jubilee, or the Jube to many, wasn't too far up 14th Street from Jubilations. By the time she got there, the show was ten minutes old. The place was only half full, but that was largely because of social distancing rules. She described the show as entertaining. She was impressed with Boudin, the silent illusionist. It was explained that because of a developmental problem, he was unable to speak. It was Marie who did all the talking. Seemed like most of my marriages.

They said that Seamus Doyle could get something from anyone. Looking back on his interview, he did wonders. He got a voice from the Silent Illusionist and a few words. It wouldn't have been much of an interview if Boudin had just sat there and said bugger all. Perhaps Doyle had indulged in a laying on hands before the show. A sort of pick up thy bed and talk.

The show quite entertained Rita. She had never seen magic before, so she was easily mystified. She was especially excited about the final illusion where Boudin dressed in Chinese robes and was teleported (not her words) from one cabinet to another and a volunteer transported from another cabinet up to the balcony. "How the fuck did he do that?" she mused. I was in no position to answer.

There was one final plus. Boudin made an appearance in the foyer to sign autographs. There wasn't much of a queue. I mean, it was 30 yards long, but remember, social distancing rules were in effect. Probably 12 people. That signature might be useful sometime later, I thought. But Rita didn't get a program. And why? They only had digital ones and her flip phone just wasn't up to that.

So, she had a good night. When I asked her what the most impressive part of the evening was, she said Marie's shoes. She was sure they were Louboutin's. Funny, that coming from someone who usually wore nothing more than runners. But that's women for you.

Red and I got home just before midnight. Rita and Jennifer were waiting for us. I've not talked about Jen yet. She was Red's girlfriend and there had been an immediate bond between her and Rita. Remember, I said that Rita had once been a pole dancer. Well, Jen was a pole dancer. I know what you're thinking. No, she was an instructor. She'd even done routines at the Stampede. They say that opposites attract. That was Red and Jen. She was fractionally under five feet and, as I mentioned, he was a big bugger. He was quiet and introverted while she was bubbly and vivacious.

Jen was a bit of an enigma. She certainly came from a slightly different social class to us. Her father was the President of an oil company and made a fortune from the oil boom that hit in the seventies. She had lived in a mansion out in the Bearspaw area. I saw it once. I'm sure there are universities smaller than that. I mean, in the U.K. they would have described her as a member of the silver spoon brigade. Now, you might think that she could have been made for life. But she was a bit of a rebel. Not that she did anything anti-social. She just wanted separation and independence from her folks and went to university to do Feminist Studies. Jesus, she could have sat down with Rita for half an hour for that. And then ten minutes with me for Masculine Studies.

And then the oil crash came. And down the toilet went her father's fortunes. Now, it wasn't as if they were having to go next door to borrow milk for breakfast. But once you are used to big money, you have a way of life to protect. Her father tried to burn down the family mansion for the insurance and got caught. And that was it. His wife was pissed off and left with what was left of the money, and Jen was on her own. Jen had little money but plenty of personality and that's why Red thought she was worth keeping around. I gather she thought the same way about him.

Anyway, it had been a successful day and Red and I bought a couple of extra-large double cheese pizzas. The girls were very careful about their caloric intake. Red would work that off in the gym. I didn't give a shit. I suppose I should have done so since I'd had one heart attack, and cardiac problems ran in the family. We finished the pizzas, and the two others went downstairs. I awoke three hours later with acid indigestion.

I said that Rita was careful about her calories, but nothing seemed to work. She was what used to be described as fully figured. Society wasn't as kind to men. We were described as fat. I would have settled for pudgy. Rita was intent on losing weight. She bought a copy of 'Slim Jim.' Dr. Jim's self-hypnosis techniques for weight loss.

Dancing with the Stars was over for the season and Rita needed a replacement activity and there it was. The following night, she suggested we could do self-hypnosis together. The program kept saying, 'You are feeling more and more relaxed, you are getting heavier and heavier.' Fuck, I wanted something that said, 'You are getting lighter and lighter.' To be fair, something worked. I didn't have acid indigestion for a week.

8
BANG BANG

I was reasonably confident that the Horsfall situation was under control. I was less confident after Louie called me on Saturday morning. He told me that there had been reports that a suspicious person had been looking at hunting knives the day before in Inglewood. Usually, this amounted to nothing. You never knew. This character had been making comments about opening somebody up. When challenged he said that he was joking but the police were called. It was too late to catch him. But it was a warning. This guy had made every effort to be caught. Was he that stupid?

I decided it might be worth an extra precaution when I went to the theatre. I'm not allowed to carry a gun, but I do have a very convincing replica. You never know, I thought. It just might come in useful. If I needed a heavy, that's where Red would enter the equation.

I thought that the only thing I had left to worry about was the dress code. Was this a posh do with formal dress? After all, it was a fundraising event for 'Seniors Surviving Covid.' I wasn't sure there could be too many left. They were popping off like flies. Nah, it was at the Pumphouse Theatres. A leather jacket and jeans would do the trick. Too cold for shorts, but I thought about it. Red felt the same way. Then I realized we hadn't bought tickets. We'd be screwed if we couldn't get in. "Marie, I'm sorry. We could have prevented your husband's murder, but we were stuck outside in the cancellation queue." Not to worry. I called the box office. They seemed glad to hear from me. Ticket sales had not been good.

The show started at 7.30 PM. We decided to take a cab. The trip to Rocky Mountain House and Red Deer had been hard on the old Civic. Besides, we thought we would arrive in style. That way, we could arrive at the front door in a taxi and avoid the water-filled potholes on the driveway.

When we walked in, there was strict adherence to the social distancing laws. There was to be no mingling in the foyer. A drink at the interval would be out of the question. When we presented our tickets, we were told that Red and I would have to social distance. This was bollocks. I told them that Red and I had been partners for years and we lived together. That seemed to work. As we walked in, Red took my hand in his. He giggled. I told him to fuck off as I pulled my hand away. An attendant hiding behind a face shield gave us a program. It smelled of disinfectant. The whole place smelled of disinfectant. We were offered a cushion. This was probably because we would be sitting for over a couple of hours on hard seats. Unless we wanted to go for a piss, there would be no movement around the theatre allowed.

The theatre was half-filled, but both the lower auditorium and balconies were open. As we sat there, the theatre slowly filled up. Because it was a charity event, there were more than a few nobs. You know the sort who wouldn't be seen dead at anything other than Theatre Calgary. I noticed a city councillor sitting in the front row. Probably there to get a photo op. I already had a few photos of him he would not be proud of. Funny how women are impressed with power. Never worked for me.

The rest of the audience was a strange mix. Everything from the elite to blue-collar to the artsy-fartsy. They were all separated by the mandatory six feet. If there was somebody there who was going to cause trouble, it was not obvious. Most people sat there pretending to read the program. The usual crap. Three pages of real information and 16 pages of adverts. Well, there were a few gaps. Some advertisers had gone out of business and the future attractions section was empty. A few adverts were projected on the red velvet curtain at the front of the stage. I guessed it hid the illusionist's props. It was cold. I was glad that I hadn't worn my shorts.

At 7.25, a group of dignitaries appeared. There were about six of them who announced their goal was the true meaning of caring. They obviously weren't from the government. They droned on about the pandemic and those who had been unfairly impacted by the virus. I mentioned to Red that we were seeing the distinguished talk about the extinguished. But joking apart, this was a serious matter to me. The aged had been dumped into nursing homes just lately. Escape was unlikely, especially if they were put on ventilators. A woman sat in the front row using oxygen. She'd probably been placed on a ventilator at one time but survived. Both Red and I agreed we had never come across anyone with Covid. For most people, the major symptoms were.... well, no symptoms.

After a few minutes, it came time for the presentation of a cheque. You've seen them before. A six-foot by three-foot piece of cardboard. Difficult to get into the automated teller, I thought. It was a cheque for twenty thousand, and they gave it to the woman in the front row. She was the president of the society. Numerous photos later, they took the cheque off her and left through the theatre doors.

A taped announcement indicated the show was about to start. No photos or videotaping allowed. Fire exits here and here. That was a bit puzzling since you could only follow the arrows on the floor and the fire exits were in the opposite direction. Perhaps if you walked backward, it might work. The lights dimmed. The show was about to start.

The velvet curtains opened on a stage which, as I had guessed, was full of equipment that could be moved into place when necessary. There was a backdrop representing what was clearly a Parisian scene. Much more impressive than downtown Medicine Hat. Marie appeared in a spotlight. She was elegantly dressed. I must admit I, too, was impressed with her shoes, though less impressed by the French accent. To be fair, she was selling something, but by now it was an irritation. She talked about Boudin and his history. How he was an orphan on the streets of Paris and was rescued from starvation by a wealthy benefactor.

Not heard this bit before. It went on and on. You get the idea. The woman at the front took out a tissue. I thought she was tearful, but she was just cleaning her oxygen mask. And then something magical. One figure who had been portrayed on the canvas slowly began to materialize. Holy shit, it was Boudin. How the hell did he do that? With a gesture from Marie, he was there. Amazing. And I'm not easily impressed. He took a bow, and the show was on. Remember, Boudin did not speak, at least not on the stage.

I hadn't seen too many magic shows before, but I reckon this was par for the course. Boudin and Marie were both equally involved. A series of simple tricks got me confused. Not difficult, I know. But how the hell did she keep producing handkerchiefs from her hands and then making them disappear again? Then she ripped up a program. I can't say that I blamed her. She hid the pieces in her fist and abracadabra. There it was, whole again. Red told me it was easy. I could buy that trick for a couple of bucks from the Edmonton Trail store. The bastard wouldn't tell me how it was done, though. Then some mind reading and card tricks and the inevitable rabbit out of a hat. Things got ramped up a bit with the woman cut in half illusion. It was OK, but it needed to be a bit more graphic. How about blood spurting out all over the stage? How about a WCB representative taking down the injury details? They used their lithe assistant Mandy for this trick. Even I knew how it was done. Let's put it this way. It wouldn't have worked with Rita. Skintight leopard leotards were not her thing. I'll say no more. And then they did the levitating lady. I can guarantee that wouldn't work with Rita without damaging Rita and the set.

And then it seemed as if the first half was coming to a climax with something special. Marie talked about the next illusion. I noted that she never actually called them illusions. She said that Boudin was about to perform an astonishing demonstration. He was going to subject himself to a firing squad. It had been done before by the amazing Chung Ling Soo. There was that name again. He had been condemned to death by the Boxers and was to be executed by a firing squad. But he had defied the bullets. At that point, Boudin appeared in an elaborate headdress and the quilted robe of a Chinese warrior. I think I'd seen something similar at the Imperial Palace.

He would get somebody to shoot him and catch the bullet on a porcelain plate. This was the only trick that Harry Houdini had refused to do. Red knew the story. Said it was too dangerous. Well, Boudin had the balls to do it. Not exactly how she described it, but you get the idea. And then Red whispered in my ear.

"That was William Robinson's last trick," he said.

'Who the fuck is William Robinson?'

"Chung Ling Soo. He wasn't even Chinese, but then Boudin hardly is."

"His last trick. He retired after that?" I mused.

"Yeah, permanently. Something went wrong."

"He died. Not embarrassment, I assume."

"Two bullets to the chest are usually fatal. It had killed others as well."

"Jesus. How do you know this shit, Red?" Then I remembered, I'd given him that book.

Then we got shushed by the audience. You know. A shut the fuck up moment.

Marie said she would need a couple of soldiers or other members of the audience who would fire a bullet at Boudin from 25 feet. Marie asked if there were any soldiers and the guy next to the oxygen lady stood up. I hadn't noticed him. I looked at Red. If there was going to be any mischief at all, this might be the moment. I stood up and said that I had been a member of the Lethbridge Rifles. It might have been a football team for all I knew. I said it with some panache. I suspect the audience believed me. Marie glared at me as I made my way to the stage. Heh, I was there to protect her husband and if he was ever in any danger, this was it. I looked at the soldier and he was far too young to be Horsfall. Marie and Boudin, for that matter, would have recognized him despite the mask.

There were two rifles on the stage. These were vintage muzzle loaders. I was given one and my soldier friend the other. He was shaking. Probably stage anxiety, but I wouldn't have wanted him pointing a weapon at me. We were asked if they were real guns. We both nodded. How would we know? Then Marie asked us to select two bullets from a bowl that was full of them. They were actually slugs, but I wasn't going to argue. We took out two bullets and then were instructed to put an identifying mark on them. The rifles were packed with gunpowder.

We gave the bullets to Marie to insert but because of Covid restrictions; she had to sanitize them. I mean, that made little sense. I'm going to shoot a bullet into your chest, but don't worry, you won't catch Covid. Boudin took position on the opposite side of the stage, and we were told to take our positions. The background music ratcheted up. The tension was supposed to mount. It did for the soldier. He looked as if he was going to shit himself. The oxygen lady's equipment beeped with every breath. And it was a case of 3, 2, 1 fire!!!!!!. We both did and watched across the stage. There was a pause. Then the porcelain plate fell to the floor. A crimson stain spread on Boudin's tunic. Marie ran to him and grasped him before he fell to the floor. The audience gasped. We heard someone scream curtains. Holy shit. I had just killed the person I was supposed to protect. I hoped Rita had deposited the last cheque we received from Marie.

9

DEADLY ILLUSION

After the shooting, there was a pregnant pause. Somebody screamed, "Get an ambulance". The curtains still did not close. Then there was the sound of an ambulance siren. Jesus, when I had my heart attack, the ambulance had taken ten minutes, not ten seconds. But it was all bullshit. Boudin smiled and stood up. He reached for his mouth and took two bullets out. If they were our bullets, they'd taste of disinfectant. He passed the bullets to Marie, who sanitized them once more. She walked over to us. "Gentleman, you marked these bullets. Are these bullets you put into the gun?" I had scored the letters BS on mine. The soldier had put an X. Those were the bullets alright. She turned to the audience and said something like "Monsieur Boudin would like to tank you for all yor elp." She then pushed us off the stage as the curtain closed. Boudin was nowhere to be seen. Probably went for a quick cig in the dressing room. If somebody had shot at me, I would have done the same.

I walked back to Red. He seemed amused. I was still a bit shaken. It's funny what goes through your mind in times like this. As soon as Boudin was shot, I wondered if this was a ruse. Perhaps Eric Horsfall didn't exist, and Marie had set me up to murder her husband. I know it was completely paranoid, but you can rule nothing out. But I quickly squashed that idea. How did she know I would volunteer to fire a shot?

Red was pissing around with his I-phone when I got back to my seat. I decided I needed a breath of fresh air or a dump or both. I needed to clear my head. There was a lineup for the bathrooms, so I stepped outside. It had started to rain heavily. One of those squalls that can easily turn into snow. There were a few people outside smoking. One of them was the lady with the oxygen tank. I assumed she was an aged survivor of Covid. She wasn't. That was her mother who had died. This woman was suffering from emphysema. 60 years of two packs a day will do that to you. I asked her if she could spare one. The consensus among the smokers. Well, they seemed to think the show had been amazing. Most of the invited guests were less impressed. They were leaving. The councillor was on his cell phone. I knew he wouldn't be going home, at least not with his own wife.

I put my mask back on and wandered back into the foyer. I took the long walk back down the corridors with their footprints, that told me which way to go. I imagined they were like those footprints that you use for dancing and tried hopping from one to another. It was like doing a quick step. Didn't think anyone was watching. They were. I bumped into the attendant, who scowled and asked me to take my seat. She gave me a few sachets to disinfect it.

One thing about an old theatre is that it is not always weather-proof. As I sat down, I noticed a bucket collecting drops of water that were leaking from the ceiling. Perhaps Marie would open the second half with a rendition of 'Singing in the Rain'. The Edith Piaf version.

Red was on the phone with Jennifer when I got back. He was talking about the last trick. Said he had recorded my involvement on his iPhone. He seemed amused. When he rang off, I told him to delete it. I didn't want to see myself on Facebook. He'd never miss an opportunity to take the piss. When I asked him what he thought about the show, he thought it was not too bad. He was surprised by the last trick. He'd just been on Wikipedia and discovered that at least 15 people had been killed doing this trick. The first was Madame De Linsky in 1820. She faced six shots and one of them hit her in the abdomen. She died two days later. 1820? Well, well. A long time before the Boxer rebellion, Monsieur Boudin.

The lights dimmed, and the second act was underway. It started in much the same way as the first act. Marie, who had on another beautiful pair of shoes, droned on about the wonderful and sensitive Monsieur Boudin, but eventually, he appeared and began a series of tricks and illusions. I don't want to bore you with a full list of his activities. Some of them were quite impressive. How on earth did he push his assistant through a sheet of glass, and it definitely was a sheet of glass. The audience had carefully examined it. And then Boudin was put in a straitjacket, put in a bag, and then sealed in what appeared to be a rigid trunk. Marie locked it with a padlock and then gave the key to a member of the audience. Unfortunately, she gave it to the emphysema lady, who immediately dropped it between the seats. The soldier next to her got on his hands and knees to find it. It added to the trick; I suppose. I just hoped they had a spare key. Then Mandy climbed on top of the trunk and lifted a curtain around herself and up above her head. There was a roll of drums for about five seconds, and then the curtain dropped. Boudin was standing on the trunk holding the curtain. Where was Mandy? Padlocked in the box, of course. Absolutely brilliant if you ask me. Then the curtain closed, and Marie addressed the audience. It was a bit more of the same.

I turned to Red. "These illusions are pretty impressive," I said. "Must take a lot of time and energy to build them."

"It doesn't," he replied. "They buy them."

"What?"

"Well, some of them might make or modify equipment for themselves. But usually, they buy them."

"How much?" I replied.

"All depends. Guys like Copperfield can afford to buy the big illusions. He might pay twenty thousand for the exclusive rights to a new illusion. That's tough competition for people like Boudin."

"So, what you're saying is that with a bit of money, I could be an illusionist."

"Now, I didn't say that. It's all in the presentation."

"What are you trying to say?"

He laughed.

"I could imagine your presentation," he said. "Ladies and gentlemen, I am but a poor orphan from Salford. You can see there is fuck all in this cabinet, but in five seconds, you'll shit yourselves."

I laughed too. And then we got the "shut the fuck up" murmur again from behind us.

Marie was droning on about Boudin. He had either gone for another cig, or he was getting changed. Look, I know you might think of me as a bit of a cynic. But you have to be in this game. Then I tuned into Marie.

"I must tell you that Monsieur Boudin is the only contemporary magician to demonstrate the following trick. It was first described as being performed in China in the third century BC by the legendary court entertainer Fu Weng, who served in the court of Zhao. To pay homage to this remarkable man, Monsieur Boudin is donning the robes that are associated with Fu Weng to recreate the ambiance of earlier times. It is a sign of respect for this most revered of all magicians."

This guy loved the Chinese influence. Perhaps his benefactors in Paris were Chinese, or he actually liked chicken feet. There's that cynicism again. But the audience seemed to be lapping this stuff up.

The curtain slowly opened to reveal two cabinets set in front of a display of Chinese semi-authenticity. The two black cabinets were separated by about fifteen feet. They were ornately decorated in what most would consider a Chinese style.

And then Boudin appeared. What a transformation. He wore a flowing black gown decorated with a gold embroidered pattern. His decor was finished with what most would describe as a black coolie hat. His face had been made up to look Chinese. No cultural sensitivity there. A Fu Manchu moustache adorned his face. I suspect he was trying to look like Fu Weng, who in reality could have been a waiter at the Imperial Palace for all I knew. To be honest, I thought he looked a bit like Peter Sellers. Still, the audience was engrossed.

Marie continued.

"Monsieur Boudin will attempt to transport himself from this cabinet over here to this cabinet here. But not only will he do that, he will attempt to transport someone else across the ether at about the same time. So, they will cross in the blink of an eye. We will need a volunteer to help us in this dangerous escapade. Let us hope there is not a metaphysical collision between the two cabinets. And remember, social distancing can mean you can be no less than six feet apart. But how to choose a volunteer? Monsieur Boudin's business card was attached to one of the programs that were distributed at the door. Now, if you could all look at your programs. Come, my friends, I know it is out there. Ah, there we are. That gentleman over there."

She was looking at a man sitting about eight rows back. Someone else I hadn't noticed. He seemed nervous, but he was holding up a business card. He wore a Yankees baseball cap and was dressed in a denim jacket and jeans. There was an insignia on the back of his jacket. It looked like a tiger's head, but I couldn't be sure. He wore a scarf around his neck. It matched his mandatory face mask. He seemed reluctant. Marie stepped off the stage and went towards him.

"Please Monsieur, please be our guest. You could be part of something historical."

She grabbed his hand and ushered him onto the stage. Once there, she remembered to sanitize her hands as she introduced him to the audience.

"Your name, Monsieur?"

"Peter ...Peter Bergman." At least I think that was what he said. It was quite muffled because of his mask.

"It is so nice to meet you, Peter. What do you do for a living?" She must have used these lines in a singles bar. I always think that's a dangerous question. What if he said he was a toilet cleaner or sewage blockage specialist or animal masturbator? Believe me, that's a job. But he didn't.

"I deal in sports and celebrity trading cards.......not much of a living these days, I'm afraid." This guy would be fucked in a singles bar.

"Do you have one of the Great Boudin?" she replied.

"You're not offering one, are you? It would have to be in good condition and signed."

"I think that could be arranged. I'm sure that Boudin will gladly sign your business card. You have a pen, monsieur."

Bergman took a pen from his breast pocket. Marie took it off him and went towards Boudin. She stopped short.

"Ah, monsieur, but only if you agree to volunteer."

Bergman nodded.

"Good, let us av a big and for this brave man." Her accent was not entirely consistent.

Boudin signed the card and passed it back to Bergman.

"Now, Monsieur Peter, I would like you to step into the box over here." She pointed towards the box on the left-hand side of the stage.

"That's stage right," whispered Red.

"Now monsieur, before you do, I would ask that you walk around the cabinet so that it is clear that there is no way in or out without being seen. I will ask Monsieur Boudin to step inside and you will see he cannot get out."

Boudin stepped into the cabinet and Marie locked him inside. Bergman walked around the box, carefully inspecting it. Boudin banged on the cabinet wall. Not too hard, though. It looked flimsy.

"There is absolutely no way out of the box. Well, not that I can see," Bergman said.

"Anything underneath? A trapdoor perhaps?"

Bergman bent down and peered underneath.

"Nothing except a bit of dust. Definitely, no trapdoor, though."

"Exactly, my friend. Now if you could exit Monsieur Boudin. I will unlock the door."

Boudin emerged from the cabinet.

"Now Monsieur Bergman, if you can get in the cabinet. She pointed to the cabinet on the left side of the stage. Perhaps take your jacket off. It can get very hot in the cabinet."

"I'll take my chances. It's a bit chilly in here," he replied. A non-compliant volunteer. Now that was a new one. But she pressed him on this and he took it off. There was muffled laughter from the audience. Bergman climbed into the cabinet. The wrong time to discover you're claustrophobic. She locked the door, or at least pretended to.

"Now I will escort the great Boudin over to the other cabinet on the right side of the stage. Ah, but before I do, we will ask him to sign his last will and testament."

"And his life insurance," whispered Red. I chuckled.

She picked up a large card from the side of the stage. It was in Chinese script. It could have said 'I loved the curried liver.' I mention this because I once ordered curried liver in a restaurant. Not sure what I got, but it tasted good and it was cheap. Anyway, there was a place for a signature and Boudin signed on the dotted line.

"If we could get someone from the audience to witness this document."

An elderly Chinese gentleman in the front row volunteered and stepped forward. He peered at the Chinese script with a puzzled almost pained look. Perhaps he was not fond of curried liver, but he signed the card, and it was placed on a string over Boudin's head.

At that moment, Red nudged me and pointed. A Police Officer had quietly stepped into the theatre. He watched intently. Perhaps someone was going to get a parking ticket. Shit, I hoped it was not Boudin. He didn't stop the show. After writing a note, the cop stopped to watch the proceedings. Boudin was obviously committing a mask violation.

"And now I will invite the great Boudin to get into the cabinet."
She pointed to the cabinet on the right side of the stage. "And your last
will and testament will go with you at all times."

Boudin bowed to the audience and stepped into the cabinet. Marie
locked it. She then walked over to the other cabinet.

"Are you still there, Peter? Please knock on the cabinet to let us
know you are not yet in the ether."

The sound of knocking was heard. It was a bit like a seance.

"We wish you a safe journey, Monsieur Peter. It is only a short
distance, but it does not always work. Who knows where you might
finish up? No need to worry, we have not completely lost anyone yet."
There were a few nervous titters from the audience

She could have said 3,2, 1, and clicked her fingers. She didn't. I
wondered what abracadabra was in Chinese. I was getting distracted.
After a few seconds, she spoke.

"Ladies and gentlemen, this is the highlight of the evening. A
moment that many of you will always remember. Some of you will not
believe but I am asking you to believe your senses. For this is real. This
is the epitome of magic and illusion. You are witnessing a true legend."

This actually seemed to come from the Lou Diamond manual for
selling used cars

"I wish she'd get on with it," said Red. "I'm dying for a piss." More
shushing. The cop seemed to have disappeared.

"One day, like Fu Weng, Boudin might still be a legend in 3,000
years. I give you the great Boudin."

The lights dimmed. A fog machine started to drone in the
background. Mist seemed to envelop the stage. Two spotlights focused
on the cabinets.

I will utter the famous magical phrase from Fu Weng, and the
transportation will begin. She clapped her hands. Nuk Yu, she
shouted. Red thought she said something else. There was a drum roll
and a clashing of cymbals.

She danced over to the cabinet on the right side of the stage and unlocked the cabinet door. Boudin was not there. She walked around the cabinet to show there was no way to get out. She closed the door. "So where could the great Boudin be?" Odd, she didn't ask where Bergman could be. My guess was that he should have been in that cabinet on the right. Perhaps he had got bored and pissed off.

Marie walked over to the cabinet on the left of the stage. She fumbled with the key. All part of the act, of course, and then slowly opened the cabinet door. Boudin stood there with his last will and testament hanging around his neck. For a moment, the audience began to clap. But after a couple of seconds, he pitched forward into her arms. She gently lowered him to the floor. A knife protruded from his back.

As this was happening, a figure emerged at the back of the theatre.

"Oh, Jesus Christ ...no!" he shouted, and then he was gone. As he disappeared, I noticed the tiger emblem on his back. This was the volunteer, Peter Bergman. How the fuck did he get up there?

When I turned back, Marie was covered in blood. So was the stage just by the cabinet. Marie was screaming. The policeman came rushing back in. The curtains were quickly closed.

Most of the audience was bemused. One of the theatre staff rushed in and ordered everyone to leave. We tried to get on the stage, but a security guard told us to fuck off. We didn't argue. As we filed out, most of the audience was in disbelief. Some thought it was all part of the show. The sound of an ambulance and police cars approaching could be heard. We left the theatre and decided to walk down to the LRT at Sunalta. There was not much conversation. We were both shocked. We could only assume that Horsfall was behind this. But how? We called Rita and Jen. They agreed to meet us at the Legion downturn. I needed a stiff drink. To hell with abstinence.

I am not sure why we thought of the downtown Legion. I would occasionally go there for lunch mid-week. The food was decent, and they had a meat raffle every Wednesday. Besides, it was on the LRT line. The girls arrived at the same time we did. It was not much of an evening. We were not sure we were talking about murder. Twenty minutes later, we were sure. It was the top story on the 11.00 PM newscast. It almost beat the latest Covid news. Boudin was pronounced dead at the theatre. A roving reporter was on the scene. He noted that a police spokesman had informed him they were searching for a suspect and that hopefully an arrest would be made soon. Then there was a brief look back on Boudin's life. They noted he was the silent illusionist. He'd certainly be silent now.

10

ANALYSIS

I didn't sleep much that night. We'd been asked to do a job and had failed. We hadn't cashed Marie's latest cheque. And I didn't intend to. Most people think of Private Investigators as not having many ethics. They don't. But we have some.

I had my first hot coffee. I needed it. We'd had a big freeze overnight, and the furnace had failed. Not much of a problem. I could always wear a fleece. But it was my tomatoes. They were done. It's always the same, isn't it? One thing goes wrong. Everything goes wrong.

Red came up. He drank decaffeinated and usually tea. You might have guessed as much. We sat there deliberating what we should do. It was almost inevitable that we'd have to talk to the police. We didn't have to wait long. Louie called. All unofficial, of course. He told us that Boudin had died almost instantly. Probably not a professional killing, but the knife had penetrated the dorsal aorta and you don't last long after that. Although the police had few clues, they assumed Bergman was responsible. Not his real name, of course. His real name was Eric Horsfall. They had found a bloodied driving license in the cabinet. It was Eric Horsfall's. It was a fake. I wondered why. And how and why had Horsfall appeared at the back of the theatre? I was puzzled.

Louie noted that there was an all-points bulletin out for Horsfall. He assured me he would be caught within 24 hours. I didn't think it would be that easy. He told us that the police knew of our involvement and would probably make a courtesy call. Why courtesy? I guess they didn't think we had much to add.

Rita was more than sympathetic that morning. She rarely got up until ten when she was not volunteering, but this morning was different. While I was talking to Red, she put together a nice breakfast. I wasn't hungry, but I wasn't going to refuse. Red would never refuse. He had the appetite of a horse. The bastard never put a pound on.

We knew that we would have to call Marie. Putting it off for a couple of days was always an option, but we decided to call her in mid-morning. We got through to her right away. She said was sitting at her desk at the warehouse. We extended our sympathies. Now I'd expected her to be overcome with grief. My character judgment was a bit off. Sure, she seemed to choke at times, but she was very focused on what had to be done. Some people can be very stoic in these situations.

Boudin was to be cremated a couple of days later. She said it was a religious thing. Not my business to ask, but I would secrete this in the back of my mind for further thought. Besides, I knew bugger all about religion.

Marie would have to put her husband's affairs in order as well as contacting his family. I suspected most of them lived in Medicine Hat and not Paris, but I had no idea. Now, I wouldn't have asked this, but Red could be blunt. He asked whether Boudin had any life insurance. That was blunt. She denied knowing much about that sort of thing, but said she would check it out. I assumed this would be our last conversation. Our involvement was over. Not so. She requested we stay on the case at least for a few days until Horsfall was found. I didn't want to raise the issue of further payment, but I told you Red was blunt. He asked about it. She didn't think this was a problem. We said we would get back to her in a couple of days.

The rest of the morning, we went over what had happened the night before. We sat down with Rita to compare notes about the fateful illusion. Remember, I said that Red had recorded the event on his phone. We went over the recording with Rita. Was there any difference between the performance at the Jube and the one at the Pumphouse? I'm not sure what we were looking for. But Rita noticed a couple of things. There was a difference between the two shows. I probably would not have noticed it. At the Jube, Boudin did not get in the cabinet on the left of the stage before the illusion. At the Pumphouse, he went into this cabinet while Bergman inspected it to see if he could get out. Not a big difference, but as Red pointed out, there had to be a reason. And there was one other thing. Bergman never appeared in the cabinet on the right. Hmmm. These things are usually tightly orchestrated. You cannot make it up on the fly. For the time being, we didn't have an answer, though if Bergman was the killer, he would hardly appear with a knife in his hand on the right side of the stage. I knew Red would worry this problem to death.

That afternoon, we received a visit from the police. It was a courtesy visit. They knew we had been looking for Horsfall. They assumed Bergman was probably Horsfall. Unfortunately, they hadn't found the murder weapon anywhere, which seemed odd. That was unusual, and it had to be found. Murderers often leave these things behind. We told the cops about the Inglewood location, but they already seemed to know that. They didn't ask about the threatening note, which was a good thing. I wasn't sure where it was. They seemed to think an arrest was imminent.

We went our separate ways that afternoon. We both wanted to think this case through. I dropped into the nearest burger joint, but when Red wanted to think things through, he would usually visit a sweat lodge. This was a truly spiritual thing for Red. It was a truly torturous thing for me. Cardiac events and sweat lodges are not a good combination. It is sometimes said that inspiration is 99 percent perspiration. And that was what a sweat lodge was all about...perspiration.

I had reached the third deck of my triple stacker when Red called. He said that he had come up with something that I should hear. I told him to get his arse over to the burger joint. He was way down south of

Calgary. It would give me time for an order of onion rings. Bugger the acid indigestion. A double milkshake would take care of that.

When Red arrived, he looked pleased with himself. I mean, he hadn't actually solved the case, but he had asked some questions that needed answering. He said that you had to think like an illusionist in these sorts of cases. The fact is that there is no magical explanation for these illusions.

"What sort of magical explanation do you mean?" I said.

"When Houdini did a similar illusion, some people believed he dematerialized his body in one location and re-materialized it in another."

"Sounds like bollocks to me."

"Precisely. There has to be a rational explanation."

"OK. I'm all ears," I said.

"So why did Boudin get into the cabinet on the left side of the stage, but only at the Pumphouse?"

"You're going to tell me, aren't you?" At least, I hoped he was. I didn't have a clue.

"The thing is, that only this way could the deceased man be Boudin," he said.

"Why so?"

"Come on, you don't really think he dematerialized and crossed over from right to left, do you?"

"OK, smart guy. So, who the fuck was the guy who they put in the cabinet on the right?"

"Don't have an answer for that, but somebody who looked like Boudin," he replied.

"Good point. Under that Coulee hat, Fu Manchu moustache, and Chinese robes, it could have been anyone. Even my mother." Red laughed.

"Precisely. That means more questions for Marie," he advised.

I was just about to order the double milkshake when my cell phone went off. It was Louie. He was breathless.

"They found Horsfall. His body was fished out of the Bow River this afternoon down by the weir."

"What weir?"

Down by the Calgary Zoo. Just opposite Inglewood. Once a body gets in there, it's going nowhere."

"Murder?"

"Nothing to suggest that. It definitely looks like a suicide."

"Suicide?" I asked quizzically.

"There were no indications of violence... well, not yet. Oh, and he had an empty bottle of sleeping pills in his pocket. We will be doing an autopsy."

"Anything else you can tell me?"

"Not now. I've got to dash. There's a news conference in a few minutes and they'll be putting out a news release. I'll get back to you later."

"Just one more thing?" I said. But he'd gone.

Red put two and two together, so I didn't have to say too much about the call. But it looked as if our hunt for Horsfall had come to an end. If Horsfall had jumped in, he wouldn't have survived long at the weir. There was essentially one way in and no way out. Plenty of people had died down there over the years, usually by accident. Even if by some miracle, he had escaped the turbulence, the water was freezing. He wouldn't have lasted more than a few minutes.

We drove home hoping to catch the news conference. We just made it. As we turned on the TV, we saw the pictures of the weir. The roving reporter described the finding of the body but was able to add something that we didn't know. Apparently, and he noted that this was unconfirmed, a suicide note had been found in Horsfall's apartment. I would have to contact Louie to see if he would tell me the contents, but it seemed as if the note also indicated responsibility for the murder.

It was all a bit sad. Two lives unnecessarily lost. It was only a matter of time before the police closed the case. I knew how it worked.

There were questions still to be asked in my view. I doubted that they ever would be.

There was one more thing spiritual in Red's life. In previous years, it would have been illegal, but not now. Cannabis smoking was now perfectly legal and Red just liked to relax that way. In fact, there was a cannabis store that had just opened in the strip mall opposite my house. I only had one requirement. If Red wanted to smoke this stuff, he'd have to go outside to smoke it. I didn't like the smell, though I occasionally used it. Rita hated it and it was her house. Oh, I didn't mention it. It really pissed Jen off. Red said it helped him think.

So, I sent Red outside to do a bit more thinking. I went on my computer to do the books and write out a few cheques. It was payday for Red and I thought he deserved a bonus. This involved a bit of tinkering. Half of Red's money was under the table. Not completely proud of that, but let's be serious. Don't most of us do that sometime in our lives?

When Red said that marijuana helped him think, he was right. A few minutes later, he came up the stairs. He had on his 'who's a clever boy' face. Jesus, that was irritating.

"What now, Red?" I tried hard not to sound irritated.

"I had another thought about the illusions," he said.

"Do tell, old friend," I replied.

"So, if you remember, Horsfall or Bergman appeared at the back of the theatre."

"That's correct."

"That doesn't make sense. And I'll tell you why."

"So, tell me. Red."

"O.K. If Horsfall was Bergman and killed Boudin one second, how the hell did he appear 5 seconds later on the balcony?"

"Perhaps he ran," I replied. It was a good question.

"Arbuckle, you know that's bullshit. He only called me Arbuckle when he was getting pissed off with me."

"So, it's bullshit. How would you explain it?"

"Well, I think it's obvious."

"Not to me, I said. "And probably not to the police."

"What about a double?"

I was tempted to say, "I don't mind if I do... a scotch will do the trick," but Red had a short temper when it came to my silly jokes.

"You mean there were two of them?"

"Exactly."

"Well, that puts things in a different light," I said. "So, who the fuck was the other guy?"

"Who knows, but it's a trick that's been used for at least a hundred years? Many of the old-time illusionists used identical twins. Houdini did. Some of the famous still do."

"Wouldn't work too well on TV, would it?"

"It did for Siegfried and Roy," he replied. And it certainly did for David.....

"David who", I replied.

"Not telling. These guys have their secrets. No need to spoil the illusion."

"Fair enough," I said

"I mentioned Siegfried and Roy because they are no longer performing."

"Siegfried and Roy. Didn't they have a second-hand store in Kensington?" I was taking the piss again. Careful Sydney. Just be careful.

"Mr. Arbuckle." Now I knew he was getting irritated. "You've never heard about Siegfried and Roy? It used to be an animal act. They used twin tigers. Let's face it, who can tell one tiger from another?"

"Good point. But there is one problem. The guy on the balcony was wearing the same clothes as Bergman."

"Not a problem. Think back. He took his jacket off before getting into the cabinet. Easy to pass the jacket onto somebody else."

"You're right. Marie may have passed it off to an assistant in the wings. The baseball cap and denim jacket could have come from anywhere."

"You saw the tiger emblem on his back. That was all that was needed for you to identify him."

"Excellent reasoning," I said though I was hardly an expert on reasoning.

"But there's another thing. If the balcony guy was the murderer, why would he even appear on the balcony at all? He'd be doing a runner, not feigning shock when he saw the body. Murderers don't usually hang around with a guilty conscience."

"That's food for thought," I said.

With that, I passed him his cheque. He looked at it and smiled.

"More than I was expecting, Sid."

He called me Sid. We were now back on the right track. My fault, I suppose. I knew I could be a bit of a dick on occasion.

"What now?" I suggested.

"Well, we should firm up our appointment with Marie for tomorrow. Too many questions need an answer. And if you could contact Louie and see if he has any more information."

"Wilco brother," I said. "What's your plan for tonight?"

"I promised to watch Jen do her pole dancing exhibition at the University. Then I thought we would catch a bite and then we're free."

"How about a game of Trivial Pursuit tonight?"

"Yep, can do, but I better check with Jen," he said.

I know Trivial Pursuit is an old farts game, but that clearly described Rita and me. We would have no idea who the last headbanger to top the charts was, but we sure as hell knew who the first man in space was. That was part of our history. We were there in spirit. It would have been even easier if we could have had a choice of names. We knew who these people were. Remembering their names could be a bit of a problem. That is why I usually played with Jen on my team. She was almost as good as Red. Those two always argued vehemently about the answers. It was a racing certainty that they would get married.

I put on my battery-powered slippers. They were supposed to give you heat when you need it. They were pretty useless, but Rita had bought them for me for my birthday. You guys know how it works. If I didn't wear them, I'd be getting heat in places. I didn't need it. I opened a can of Guinness, for the iron, of course. My doctor had recommended it because of my anemia. Who was I to argue? We were having leftovers that night. I decided to have another Guinness. Thought it might improve my appetite.

I was slipping into unconsciousness when my cell phone woke me from my slumber. It was Louie. He had time to talk. He told me that the suicide note was quite explanatory. It essentially said that Horsfall had no regrets about the murder. He had done the crime. Being caught was not an option. He would take the easy way out. I asked him what the message was printed on. He said it was on notepad paper. I asked because I had just remembered putting the first threatening letter in my glove compartment. I could compare them. He also noted that there had been a positive identification of Boudin. Two or three people other than his wife had positively identified him. A DNA analysis was deemed to be unnecessary. I knew the score. Save on cost wherever possible. Louie said that he was certain that the case would essentially be closed in the morning. And then he said something very interesting. He said that he was still uncomfortable about the case and wondered if we could join forces to further investigate.

I better tell you a bit more about Louie. I had known him for years. He was originally from somewhere in the middle of Europe. If pushed, Romania comes to mind. He had fled the country during the Ceausescu regime and had never gone back. It was always his ambition to join the police force, and he did about the same time as I did. Great sense of humour but a bloody awful accent. He constantly butchered the language. Sometimes I think he did it on purpose. But you couldn't take the piss out of him. He was a great bear of a man. He used to wrestle, but not quite in the same way that Red had. Greco-Roman, I think he called it. I got to know Louie through the police, and we always got on well. He was like me.... no bullshit. But one thing cemented us. The 1990 earthquake in Romania. His parent's house was destroyed. They were very poor and essentially fucked. I helped organize a fund, and we saved the day for them. He never forgot. Even when I left the force, I would occasionally meet with him for a beer. He'd always give me a bear hug and remind me about my zip. And he'd always pay.

I didn't go into what his misgivings were. That could wait a couple of days. Rita and I had supper and waited for Red and Jen to arrive. Rita was like a bloodhound. She said she could detect the aroma of cannabis. I told her they were having a controlled burn at the adjoining rubbish dump. I poured her a large gin, and she forgot all about it.

When Red and Jen arrived, we got the Trivial Pursuit out. But we never got around to playing it. The talk inevitably revolved around Boudin's murder. And then to Boudin's show. What did we think about it? After a few light beers, I can get talkative and, frankly, a tad silly. I said that the show was too serious. It needed a bit more levity. They all asked me what I would have done differently. I thought about sawing the lady in half. It needed a bit more panache. I would have called it "Sawing my mother-in-law in half" That didn't go down too well. Rita and I were only common law, but her mother was a real gem. They say the value of a diamond is a function of its flaws. That was why she was a real gem. Never told Rita or her mother that. I also had a few other ideas. When Marie did the trick where she ripped up the paper, I would have started it differently. I would have said that I had ripped up a letter from the Canadian Revenue Agency. Now I would put it back together. I would then bring out the letter. You are being audited, it said. I would have screamed "fuck that" and ripped it up into pieces again.

We decided to defer the Trivial Pursuits. It had been a good day for Red and me, and Jen's demonstration had gone well. Besides, Red was looking frisky. How did I know? Let's call it a trade secret. We decided to call it a night. Rita had tried a new perm. Her hair was in curlers. No use me feeling frisky tonight. I quickly went downstairs and asked if I could borrow the book on Chung Ling Soo. The one I had given Red for his birthday. He passed it out to me. "Indian Giver," he said. We both pissed ourselves laughing.

Reading in bed for me was usually not a good idea. The book would usually drop out of my hand within two minutes, and I would be in the land of nod. But this Chung Lin Soo was an interesting character. Not his real name, as I mentioned before. This fella, William Robinson, had taken over the persona of a real Chinese illusionist, Chung Lin Foo. And the world believed him. Good makeup and the ability to bullshit in gobbledygook Chinese can do that. It was how he did his illusions that piqued my interest. And then Rita started snoring. I turned the light out. I was to wake up again at 4.00 AM. I needed a piss. Just another senior moment. I decided to continue reading and there it was, in black and white. The Proteus illusion. I knew how Boudin's illusion was done. Just wait until I told Red. Rita started snoring again. I slept on the couch the rest of the night.

11

LOUIE

Although we had suggested meeting Marie the next day, we cancelled it until the day after. There were a couple of reasons for this. It was a Sunday and though I am certainly not religious, you have to take others feeling into account. Perhaps Marie was still grieving. Perhaps not. But there were several other reasons. I always liked to pop down to the Imperial Palace on Sunday morning for Dim Sum. The dam best dim sum in town. We usually went with the girls, but we had arranged to link up with Louie that morning and we'd pay this time. After that, we had to visit with a pal of Reds. He lived on the Tsu Tina reserve. He had told Red that he had an old bus that he was trying to get rid of. Sure, it was clapped out, but Red thought it might be a bit more appropriate for surveillance than Walid's Falafel piece of shit. I mean, it wasn't a bad thought. Let's face it, you see school buses parked all the time. Well, perhaps not in Pump Hill. No, it wasn't perfect. The engine needed a bit of work and there were no seats, but a deal is a deal. And the deal? To provide help on a security issue that was developing on the reservation and the bus was ours. We'd pop down to the reserve a little later on.

There was always a queue at the Imperial Palace. I'd never queue for anything except at that restaurant. I hate wasting time. Louie had not yet arrived and when he did, I knew he would eat the fucking place out. What a way to start the day. A Tsingtao beer (non-alcoholic) at eleven 'o'clock in the morning and plates of shrimp balls...

my favourite. Red had given me the nickname "Shrimp Balls" over the years. I assumed it was because I liked shrimp balls, but it had another meaning. That was, perhaps, part of the joke.

After about ten minutes, Louie arrived. It was the grand entrance. I mean, you couldn't miss him. He knew the manager. Hell, he seemed to know everybody in the place. I thought Red was a big bugger, but Louie was in another domain. He planted himself at our table, smiled, and immediately tucked into the calamari before he said anything.

"God see my friends this morning," he said.

Well, he didn't actually say it that way. It was a tortured mix of consonants. I've translated his comments below.

"I understand you've got some doubts about the Boudin case."

"Nothing concrete. Just a feeling."

"What do you mean?" replied Red quizzically.

"Just a few unusual things. Marie just didn't seem that upset when I interviewed her."

"Perhaps she is just stoical or in denial," I said. I was playing devil's advocate.

"At one point she seemed to cry. She put her hands over her face, but I found her looking through her fingers at me like this."

"Anything else, Louie?" I replied.

"Yeah, when I asked her about life insurance, she said she didn't know."

"It's possible she didn't know, but I'm like you. I doubt it. Wives usually know."

"And I just had this feeling...a sort of second sense," he said.

"You're not suggesting that she was behind his murder," Red asked

"Not quite yet."

"Who knows, she might have taken out a million-dollar policy on him last week. It's happened so many times before," I countered.

"Wouldn't prove murder, though."

"It would certainly provide a motive, Louie," I replied.

"Anyway, my good friends, I'll let you interview her about the murder. See what you think."

"We're hoping to see her tomorrow afternoon after the cremation," Red said.

"A bit soon for that. Not like that in Romania. Wait a few days"

"Is there any way you can join us when we interview Marie?" I replied.

"Nah, I'm in Edmonton tomorrow. Something to do with the new Covid crisis."

After that, we essentially stuffed ourselves. Louie's appetite knew no bounds. He'd already demolished several plates when his cell phone rang.

"Gotta go," he said. "Big fuck up on Deerfoot Trail." The last part of his breakfast spilled from his mouth.

With that, he got up and was about to leave when he took a couple of business cards from his wallet.

"I've got a new cell phone number. It's on my card."

He gave a card each to Red and me. And there it was. Decebal Vladimirescui. Now you see why we called him Louie, though fuck knows where the name Louie came from. Perhaps he just looked like a Louie.

Once he had gone, Red I began to focus on the Boudin situation. I told him about the Proteus Illusion. Holy shit. He'd never heard of it. That was a first. I even gave him the page where I'd found it. He asked me to describe it.

"You know, people say it's all done with mirrors," I said. He nodded knowingly.

"Show me how it was done. I better tell you I do have my own theory," he replied.

Of course, he did. I showed him exactly what I thought had happened.

I took the small dishes that had held the soya sauce and cleaned them with my napkin. I placed them left and right.

"These are the two cabinets," I said

"I see."

I placed a shrimp ball on the left side plate. I place another shrimp ball on the right-side plate. I then picked up another shrimp ball in my hand and doused it with soya sauce. I placed it just in front of the left-side plate.

"Now the shrimp ball with soya is Boudin. Remember that."

"I'll try not to eat it." He laughed.

"Watch very carefully," I said. "Now, remember, this is all done with mirrors."

"I think I got the message."

"So, Boudin goes into the cabinet on the left." I placed the shrimp ball in my hand on the left plate in front of the other shrimp ball.

"That's Boudin in front," said Red

"Correct. But you can't see the other shrimp ball from the audience. It's behind a mirror."

"If you say so."

"So Boudin moves to the back of the cabinet and is replaced by the other shrimp ball, who then comes to the front."

"And this one looks exactly like Boudin except he isn't doused in soya sauce?" I gave him a cold, hard stare.

"Exactly. So Boudin's double comes out and eventually goes to the plate on the right."

I then placed another shrimp ball on that plate.

"Why do you need two shrimp balls on the right-side plate?" Red asked. "We never saw anybody else over there."

"Good point."

I took the second shrimp ball away from the right plate and ate it.

"Now let's pretend this meatball is Bergman."

I stole a meatball from the next table that had been left uneaten. I then placed it in front of the left side plate.

"Now, Bergman gets in the cabinet or the left side plate."

"I see. And the meatball changes places with Boudin. Boudin moves to the front, and the meatball goes behind the mirror," Red said.

"Then the Boudin look-alike shrimp ball goes behind the mirror on the right side. Abracadabra, he's gone."

"I think I'd sort of worked that out," muttered Red. "So let me summarize what you are saying."

"Boudin goes into the cabinet on the left side of the stage as we look at it. He then changes place with a Boudin lookalike who has been hidden behind a mirror. This guy then leaves the left side cabinet and goes into the right side cabinet. Then Bergman, the guy from the audience, gets in the left side cabinet and changes places with Boudin. The Boudin lookalike goes behind the mirror on the right side and abracadabra. We assume Boudin has disappeared. The real Boudin will be exposed in the left side cabinet, but sadly, he now has a knife stuck in his back."

"Correct. And that seems to suggest that Bergman must have been the killer."

"And sadly, he's dead now."

"You got it. And remember. It's all done with mirrors," I said. "Let me show you."

I then proceeded to show Red how mirrors were used in the illusion. It was very simple but quite clever. It was an illusion that was at least one hundred and fifty years old. Some people had used this illusion without the cabinet doors. I know you're waiting for the explanation. Don't be offended, but you can bugger off. Call it professional etiquette but there are illusionists out there still plying their trade. I really don't want to spoil their gig. You can look it up for yourself. So, no and I'm sticking to it.

I ate the two shrimp balls and a meatball and asked for the bill. As always, it was quite reasonable. We left the restaurant and had gone no further than fifty feet when Louie called.

"Not good news this time," he said. "They still haven't found the murder weapon."

"Find the knife and find the prints. Don't remember Bergman wearing gloves. Easy." I replied.

"We have a few Albert Epsteins in Homicide who might work that out. But I'll mention it." He chuckled.

"Anything else?" I said.

"No, boss." And he was gone.

I then drove down to the reservation and met with their head of security. The bus was as advertised. We didn't know about the graffiti on the side. Much of it was quite offensive. I could put up with the "Oilers Suck" but some of the other stuff went a bit too far. We'd have to drive it home that day. Driving it was difficult. There was no seat, but Red sat on a waste bin and managed to get it back to my place. We could go down to the Auto Dump and find a couple of seats later.

When we got home, we called Marie to confirm the meeting the next day after the cremation. It would be the last cheque we would expect. I took a couple of antacids and decided that I would finish the Chung Lin Soo book. No go. Red asked for it back. He wanted to check out the Proteus illusion for himself.

12

THE WAREHOUSE

We arrived at the Boudin warehouse the next afternoon. You had to buzz from outside to be let in. There had been a small reception for friends and acquaintances just before we got there but most of them must have gone back to Medicine Hat. It was clear that there had not been many. A few wine glasses and cheese plates in the waste bin gave the game away. The two cabinets from the show were sitting in the middle of the floor which was surprising since I would have thought they still would have been evidence. The wicker trunk had been moved to the side. A bible rested on the top. There was a skylight above our heads through which the dying afternoon light could be seen filtering in. You could hear the rain pounding on. It. That would soon be snow. There was a door that I suspect led to a warehouse and the biggest clue. There was a sign on the door that said warehouse.

Marie was formally dressed in a black suit and was going through a few sympathy cards that were sitting on her desk. She invited us in and asked us to take a seat. As we did so, her phone rang. It was an old-style wall phone. She turned away from us as she answered. Red pointed to her desk. There were two steaming cups of coffee sitting there. Perhaps we had interrupted something. Red gave the what gives look. I'd seen it so many times before.

When she put the phone down, she told us it had been the crematorium. They had phoned to ask what she should do with her husband's ashes. She seemed a bit non-plussed and suggested that they deliver them to her. She said she would consider scattering them in the mountains. And then she ended the call. She said she was grieving and was simply too upset to talk anymore.

Well, she didn't seem that upset and, in fact, seemed quite business-like when she put the phone down. So, I didn't feel too bad about asking her a few questions. Of course, she didn't have to answer. I would try to seem tactful and sensitive. Not one of my strong points, I'm afraid.

"Sorry to be disturbing you, Marie, on this very difficult day, but we just popped in to pick up our last cheque." Not very sensitive that. But she didn't seem that upset.

"Of course, Mr. Arbuckle. I have the cheque written out to you." No cash this time, but I wasn't going to argue.

She opened the desk drawer and took out a cheque.

"I have filled it out with a bit of a bonus on the top."

"Very generous of you," I said. And then I noticed something. "This is signed by Boudin," I remarked.

"No conspiracy here, Mr. Arbuckle." She laughed. "Boudin alone signed all our cheques, including my recent cheque to you. He signs quite a few at a time. I just fill in the details. I probably should destroy the rest."

"That's true," agreed Red. I'm surprised you didn't notice that, Sid. He sat there smiling and rolling his eyes.

I decided it was time to change the subject.

"I don't suppose you'd mind if my colleague Red looked at some of your equipment. He has a passionate interest in illusions."

"Yes, but I would ask him to be very careful. The equipment could be damaged very easily. And our secrets are precious. Confidentiality is important."

Before Red had time to move, the door to the warehouse opened, and a familiar face emerged. He didn't know we were there.

"I'm sorry darling........" He stopped when he realized we were there. "I'll pop back in a moment."

I'm not suggesting that Marie looked embarrassed. Slightly un-comfortable might have best described it. She was quite aware of the glance that passed between Red and me.

"I believe you have met my colleague Stephen before. He can be really quite effusive." I didn't know what that word meant.

"Meaning?"

"Stephen's very artistic. Darling is a very common term between theatre people." She was digging an even bigger hole. Why did she need to explain?

I looked at Red again. I didn't try to hide it. She had to notice.

"Besides, Stephen plays for the other team," she said.

"The other team?" I said. "Oh, you mean he's........."

"That's exactly what I mean. But this is the arts, and we are very accepting," she said.

"And we are Private Investigators, and we are very accepting as well," I replied.

She should have dropped the issue there and then. But she didn't.

"His partner is a well-known member of one of our professional sports teams. He's very discrete about it, of course."

Time to change the subject. She had made her point, just not in the way she intended.

"I'm sorry to bring this up, but how has all this left you finan-cially?"

"Why are you asking me these questions?'

To be honest, I was talking to a police officer who knows about the case and he had a couple of questions to ask you. He wondered if I could ask them. Better than him coming down here just for a couple of questions. Anyway, the case should be closed within the next 24 hours.

"I hope it is. So, let me answer your question. I think you might say I will be left comfortable, but I won't be able to live an extrava-gant life. These have been difficult times for illusionists. One minute they are very popular, the next moment you're working in a cheap nightclub. A good agent can't even help you these days. TV has destroyed everything."

"And right now?"

"A bit of a trough. But one has to be resilient."

"Did you have anything to gain from your husband's death?"

"If that's an accusation, Mr. Arbuckle, it is......"

"No, no, not an accusation at all."

"I believe my husband did have a life insurance policy. I have no idea exactly how much. I don't even know if I was the beneficiary, though I'd obviously be surprised if I wasn't. I suppose I could find out. I've not had time since his .... his...."

At that point, she stopped to wipe away what appeared to be non-existent tears. She did not have a tissue. I thought about offering her my handkerchief but thought better of it. Didn't want to lose another client

"So, who else might have benefited?" said Red

"Look, we all know that Horsfall committed the murder.".

"Seems like it," I replied. "Just tying up loose ends. He might have been representing someone else's interests, of course."

"I can't think of anyone. My husband had been married before, but it ended acrimoniously."

"They all seem to these days," said Red as he looked at me. He smiled. I knew that was a bit of a dig.

"So, his ex-wife might have had a motive, then?" I said.

"I'm sure she did at one time."

"Meaning?"

"She's been dead for quite a few years...suicide, I'm afraid."

"What do you propose to do now?"

"Look, Mr. Arbuckle, my life is over. I have lost my husband, and I have lost my stage career. There are not many opportunities for a magician's assistant that could keep me in the middle-class lifestyle I have become accustomed to."

"What about all the equipment? The illusions?"

"Who knows? I suppose I could sell them. They would be worth something to other illusionists."

"Anyone contact you yet?"

"As a matter of fact, yes. Some famous names you might have heard of. It would be painful to see others use them."

"Any other family members that might benefit. Children?" said Red.

"Look inspector you've asked your couple of questions. I really am busy. And there were no children."

"I think that should do it then," I said.

"Oh, there is just one thing that puzzles me," said Red

"And that is?" She glared at Red.

'Horsfall was very lucky to get the marked program. How did he do that?"

"I wondered the same thing," she said. "The fact is, he didn't have the marked program. We had forgotten to put it out. Most people are reticent to volunteer. Horsfall was not." For something that was so reliant on precision, this would have to be more than careless, I thought to myself.

"One last question," I said. "And I promise you it will be the last."

"I will take you at your word, Mr. Arbuckle."

"Tell me a bit more about Mr. Horgan."

"What do you need to know?"

"His background. How long have you known him?'

"I have known Stephen for fifteen years. He has designed and con-structed some of the world's most amazing illusions."

"But not with you?"

"Sadly, that is true," she said. "He has worked with some of the greatest illusionists in the world. He spent a considerable amount with such names as David..........You can fill in the blanks."

"Worked with them. What did he do?" I said.

"Devised illusions. It was he who was responsible for moving the Taj Mahal."

"You mean the restaurant on Macleod Trail?" I queried.

"I'm sorry. He's an idiot," said Red. I remember that illusion. He made the real Taj Mahal disappear."

"So, he was good," I said. "Why on earth did he agree to work with you?"

"I hope you're not being pejorative, Mr. Arbuckle."

"Per...per what?" What the fuck was she talking about?

"She means insulting," said Red.

"No. Not at all. You got him at short notice when Horsfall left you."

"He was semi-retired and there were Covid travel restrictions. Money wasn't an issue. He had known Boudin for many years. Let's call it a personal favour."

"Of course, he would know how all the illusions were performed."

"Obviously he would. It might surprise you I was pretty much in the dark. Boudin liked to keep his secrets."

"It surprises me," Red added. "It surprises me a lot."

"How did Stephen get on with Horsfall?" I asked.

"It was brief and acrimonious, but you better ask Stephen when you see him."

"We'll do that," I replied. "Anyway, we better be off." I motioned to Red that we should leave.

Before we could move, the entrance door buzzed. It was the crematorium delivering Boudin's ashes. We went down the corridor and passed the courier, who was holding a gold-embossed box.

As we got into the car, Red mumbled something under his breath.

"What was that?" I said.

"That's one box even Boudin won't be able to escape from."

I thought the remark was in extremely bad taste. I pissed myself laughing.

13
SCHOOL BUS

We dropped off at the Dog and Duck pub on the way home. It was an English-style pub just off Macleod Trail. It had good beer and some traditional English cuisine. Well, haggis was not English, but you get the idea. Rita was going to be out tonight. Bingo night. She described it as 3-D bingo. Don't know whether she was taking the piss or not, but that's where she was. I opted for sausages and black pudding with mashed potatoes. I washed it down with a non-alcoholic beer.

Red and I needed to talk. There was something else going on here. Marie had simply been unconvincing. There was a real element of bullshit about her answers. As we sat there we took turns to question her credibility. Despite her claims to the contrary, she simply did not play the role of grieving wife plausibly. I'm more distressed when I misplace my credit card. I've seen the false tears routine too many times. While I realize some people can go into a state of denial, that is the exception rather than the rule. And then there was the issue of life insurance. Marie was not the sort of person who would not know about this. She could probably tell you how much interest she paid on her last credit card statement.

She said she had been working with Boudin for many years, but she did not know how the illusions were done. Give me a break. That's absurd. Perhaps she thought that woman was actually sawed in half. Did she think we were idiots? I'd prefer it if you didn't comment about that.

And then there was Stephen Horgan. We'd have to talk to him. Marie's excuses for the 'darling' comment were just not plausible. And as for playing for the other team and being involved with a professional sports star, this sounded likely a hastily concocted story. And why? Because both Red and I assumed that she was having an affair with him. I mean you just know, don't you? But what did this mean in the big picture? Who knows, but it didn't stop us from speculating.

How did the apparent affair impact the murder? It might have been irrelevant, but it might have pointed the finger of suspicion elsewhere other than Horsfall. But how? Was this the case of a jealous lover who wanted to get rid of Marie's husband? And how would this involve Horsfall? We just didn't know, but we were determined to find out. If possible, we would have to talk to Horgan. It might be worthwhile surveilling him. Red agreed. Who was going to do it? I had an idea.

Jen had always expressed an interest in helping us out with surveillance. Why not? But how? She had plenty of spare time. Her University classes were suspended because of the ongoing Covid crisis. She had plenty of spare time.

Red asked her to meet us, and she was there within 20 minutes. She took little convincing. We wanted to know more about Horgan. Perhaps she could follow him. Marie and Horgan had never met her. We decided it might be an idea to stake out the warehouse. Hell, we had no idea what we were looking for. There might have been nothing. But there was something not right here. We decided to go back to the warehouse and have a look around. The lights were still on, so there was obviously somebody inside. We went around the back of the warehouse and Horgan's motorbike was still there. Now, I'm no expert on these things, but this looked like a clapped-out Suzuki 250 cc job. Not the sort of thing an independently wealthy man or even a clapped-out private eye would consider.

We decided that we should use our new super sophisticated stakeout vehicle to watch the warehouse. Who the hell would suspect a school bus? Jen volunteered to do the surveillance that night. I didn't think it was that urgent, but we took her up on the offer. Red drove back to our house and picked it up. It was still a bit limited, seat-wise. There was now a captain's chair with wheels on for the driver. You had to drive slowly. Any sudden stops would have put you through the windscreen. We'd also put a deck chair on the passenger side. Not perfect for observation. All you could see from the outside was through the windscreen. The side windows were filthy, so that was a plus.

The real need, in my view, was to somehow get into the warehouse. Now I'm not suggesting something illegal. As I have pointed out previously, sometimes people accidentally leave doors open. You never know. And obviously, it had to be when Marie and Horgan were not there. That could come later.

We parked the bus on the spare ground to the side of the warehouse about forty yards away. We could see who came and went. It was going to be a chilly night for Jen. I offered her my battery-powered slippers. She refused. I may have to re-gift those things next year.

We told Jen to keep in touch if anything happened. She could call at any time, although I sort of hoped that she didn't. I don't do too well when my sleep is interrupted. And she didn't call until 8.15 AM the following morning. But there was one notable incident to report. About fifteen minutes before she called, she was woken up by banging on the door. When she looked out, there was a lineup of kids waiting to get on the bus. She told them to bugger off. We wouldn't have to wait too long for the complaints from the Calgary Board of Education to start.

I drove down to the warehouse with Red to go over what might have happened during the night. Horgan and Marie had left during the night. Jen admitted she dozed off at about midnight for a few minutes. It was what we had not asked Jen to do that night that was so inter-esting. She was aware of the skylight above the office and thought it might provide some insight into what was going on. The only problem was that it was on the roof. Now I told you she was athletic. The drain pipe up to the roof was not an issue. So up she went. She cleared some of the dust off the skylight and peered down. There was not much to see at first. Then Horgan came in and the two hugged. She described it as passionate. They then left. There was not much beyond that, but it answered all our questions. All right, some of them.

I was delighted about Jen's 'go get em' attitude but Red was less impressed. He was worried that she might have hurt herself. That was reasonable. He was also concerned that someone could have stolen the bus while she was on the roof. That was not reasonable. He must think there is a huge secondhand market for school buses with no seats. Except for landfills, I suspect not.

We decided to go for breakfast at a greasy spoon on Blackfoot Trail. You get to know these places when you're doing surveillance. They don't look that good from the outside. Inside, you get a darn substantial breakfast for half the price of the big boys. Usually, it's cash only, but who cares?

Our first goal was to get some coffee into Jen. We'd get her caffeinated for just as long as it would take to discuss what she had observed. She was less focused on that because she wanted to know what the next step was. The girl had caught the surveillance bug. I know it's a bug. I caught it years before and there's no vaccine.

She described the intimate connection between Marie and Horgan. I mean, for those with dirty minds, not that intimate. Passionate doesn't necessarily mean hot sex. Even so, this was hardly kissing your sister. The issue was what to do next.

Before my steak and eggs had arrived, we'd come to some conclusions. There was clearly something going on here. We had to get into the warehouse. But how? There was a good security system at both entrances, but Jen, in her last gasp of consciousness, came up with the perfect solution. You could get in through the skylight. She said we could easily climb down to the floor. Without turning up my pacemaker into the do not resuscitate zone, any attempt would not include me. It would have to be her and Red. When would be the issue?

We also left the bus where it was. There was no need to move it, and we would continue to surveil the warehouse. We had only one concern. It was parked about 50 yards from a wrecker's yard. We didn't want them taking advantage of a seemingly abandoned bus. Red had another great idea. We should put a 'For Sale' sign on it. Seemed like a good idea at the time.

What was the plan going forward? We put our heads together and came up with the following. Calling Louie was essential. Let's see if he had anything on Horgan. We thought it might be useful to trail Horgan to see what he was up to. Now that Boudin was dead, that was a big issue. What was he up to?

When were we going to break into the warehouse ...I mean, find an open door......and see what was in there? If we could be sure there was nobody there, the following night was a possibility. We'd have to do it in the middle of the night, and we would have to check that there were no security cameras nearby.

Jen said she could get back to the bus after four to continue surveillance. If Horgan was still there, she could follow him to his home. She would need some sleep first. She had nothing urgent to do. Because of the Covid situation, she had done some online courses with Athabasca University. This was an off-campus university. I tried it once. Didn't have the discipline, but she did. It was time to get her home. I'm sure she was asleep before her head hit the pillow.

Red did first duty on the bus that morning. He saw Marie drive up. Horgan was already there. And nothing much happened. On reflection, that was not exactly true. Three people came by hoping to buy the bus 'as is.' He had to tell them all that it had just been sold. Since we had got it for nothing, there was likely to be a profit to be made in the future. Not much, but profit is not a dirty word.

I was going to be tied up for the rest of the day. I had to give evidence in court that afternoon for the prosecution side. That was usually a waste of time. By the time they got to me, the guilty had usually thrown themselves on the mercy of the court. Still, I couldn't complain. A few hundred bucks for doing the Sun crossword was my sort of work.

I had quite forgotten to call Louie until late afternoon. He had checked up on our friend and while the results were not exactly earth-shattering, they were interesting. He was less self-made than self-destructive. Horgan had been married three times. I knew how self-destructive that could be. He was still paying child support. Correction, he was supposed to be paying child support in the States but wasn't. And his credit rating was in the crapper. No other evidence of malfeasance. No criminal cases, no reported acts of violence...nothing. Sure, he had been involved with other illusionists, but most did not last too long. That was it. No evidence of any gay alliances. But who knows? That's perhaps why his marriages failed. It sometimes happens.

Marie and Horgan were still there in the warehouse until about four, when Jen drove up to take over. At least we assumed they were there. Her BMW was out front, and his motorbike was out back. We decided that we would watch one more night before finding that open door the following night. I might have suggested that night, but it was darts night for me at the Legion. I couldn't miss that. Rita had her bingo; I had my darts.

I was halfway through a game that night when my phone went off. I almost ignored it, but it was Louie with an update. He told me that while Horgan did not have any reported instances of violence, there were rumours that he might have been responsible for the death of his first wife. So, he was potentially capable of violence. Next dart, I threw a double top to win the game. I need good news more often.

When I got home, I still had not heard from Jen. I sat with Rita, who was watching the Kardashians. Not my sort of stuff, but I could tolerate it for a few minutes. When Red came up the stairs, he wondered whether I had heard from Jen. We were both a bit worried. It was time to call her. When we did, she said was on her way home but had some interesting information. She then rang off. I would have to put up with Kardashians a few minutes longer.

Jen arrived about ten minutes later. We could have talked upstairs, but the Kardashians were about to hit an exciting moment if you can believe that. Rita would have made a shushing sound, or worse if we had interrupted. We went downstairs.

'Well, young lady, what have you come up with?'

That was not the way I should have put it. The young lady bit I mean. I could be socially insensitive at times, but apart from a frown, I got away with it.

"I found out quite a bit about Mr. Horgan tonight."

"And you're going to tell us," said Red.

"I need a stiff drink first."

I looked at Red. This was quite unlike Jen. She didn't drink. And then she started laughing.

"Just shitting you guys."

Now she was even talking like a private eye.

"Very good. So, for fuck's sake, tell us what happened."

"Well. Horgan left at about six on his motorbike. I followed him in my car. He stopped off for a drink at a pub on 17th Ave."

"Southeast, or southwest?" I said.

"Southeast." Interesting neighborhood. Let's say it was deprived. When I was a cop, it certainly wasn't deprived of crime. I used to live there, so I knew.

"Which pub?" asked Red.

"No idea, but he came up to me and asked me if I wanted something to drink."

"What do you say?"

"I told him I was dating the drummer in the band."

Holy shit, I didn't think they used that excuse anymore. They did in my day.

"There really was a band playing?" said Red.

"There was. It wasn't a great excuse, I know. The drummer was a pimply adolescent with greasy hair and noticeably bad teeth."

"Sounds like the British invasion. I was there," I said.

We all laughed

I didn't hang about. I immediately left to get into my car. I was stopped at the door by a mask marshall. I had walked into the bar without my mask. I could have been done for a thousand bucks, but he let me off with a warning. You could go to jail for that sort of thing these days. Then I sat in my car waiting for Horgan to come out. He did so after about an hour carrying a six-pack.

"And then?" Red asked.

"He went about six blocks and went into ......I'm not sure how to be kind about this.........an economic apartment."

"A flea pit?" I said.

"Not a description I would use," she said. "But I can't disagree. I would have looked through the window, but I didn't want to risk being caught."

"A flea pit for someone with no money issues. Isn't that what Marie suggested?" said Red.

"That's true," I replied. "But some millionaires have been known to live in poverty. Look at me." Everyone chuckled.

"Anyway, let's see what we've got here," said Red.

"A cesspit of lies," I replied. I could be quite descriptive when I put my mind to it.

"You mind if I summarize the facts we have," said Red.

"No problem, the floor is all yours," I replied.

"Boudin, it seems, gets knocked off by this guy Horsfall, who is said to be pissed that he wasn't getting enough credit. He tries to extort Boudin, but they fuck it up. Horsfall then kills Boudin and then apparently commits suicide. But while this is going on, Marie appears to be having it away with her construction assistant. Not in her class and someone who she says plays for the other team."

"Perhaps he played both sides," said Red.

"We can only speculate," I replied.

"Could it be that Horgan wanted to take over the show from Boudin?" said Red. "He had access to the illusions. He had a ready-made assistant. Might call himself the second coming of the maestro. And Marie tells one lie after another. Too many to recount. The question is why."

"You don't believe the official line," said Jen. "What about you, Sid?"

"I'm not convinced."

"And there is still one thing that bothers me," said Red. "I know I've mentioned it before, but how the hell could Horsfall get from the scene of the murder up to the balcony in less than two seconds? Unless he was an expert knife thrower who could throw the knife from the balcony, get it to do a 180, and fly it through a closed cabinet. It's impossible. There had to have been two people involved. There simply had to have been. And surely Marie would have recognized Horsfall."

"He was pretty well disguised," I said.

"With the mask and baseball cap, I see your point."

"Seen it before," I said. "The police do a damn good job, but it's always nice for them to solve a case. They probably think they have solved it. Move on, no questions asked. This is not Perry Mason anymore."

"Who?" said Jen.

"Who hasn't heard of Perry Mason?" I replied.

"Ninety-nine percent of the population," said Red. Fuck, I really was getting old.

"So, what's the game plan team?" I said.

"I think we surveil again tomorrow."

"What will that achieve, Red?"

"Probably nothing. If we go in, we have to be sure there is no one there."

"What do you think, Jen?"

She was fast asleep. It had been a long day.

14

POOR ERIC

This was going to be the day everything happened. I just didn't expect it to happen so early. Breakfast was a strong coffee and a bowl of all-bran. Hate that shit, but it was doctor's orders. Hell, I usually ignore doctor's orders. It was about seven in the morning. I was reading the newspaper or what was left of it. Covid had seen to that. Rita was droning on about the latest edition of Dr. Pimple Popper. I tried to look interested. She had just gotten to the climax of the episode when my cell phone went off. Saved by the bell. Who the fuck would call at this time of the morning? It was Louie. I told Rita to finish the story later. Hopefully, much later.

"Louie, do you know what time it is?"

"No fucking idea. You tell me."

"My sundial doesn't work in the dark," I said. I expected the big guffaw and there it was.

"I got some interesting news this morning, my friend. Fatal accident in St. Hubert."

"Where's that?" I said.

"It's part of Montreal."

"But why is that interesting?"

"It was who was killed that's interesting."

"For fuck's sake," I said. "Who was killed?"

"Brace yourself. It was somebody called......Mr. Eric Horsfall."

"Yeah, but there must be quite a few Eric Horsfalls in Canada," I replied.

"But not many with some magical equipment and posters of Boudin on the back seat. It appears as if he had been in Montreal for a couple of months." This was definitely a 'what the fuck' moment.'

"Holy shit!" I said. "But who the hell committed suicide a few days ago, and why would he be stealing Horsfall's name?"

"Your guess is as good as mine. But I'll definitely be following this up. Fingerprints, DNA, and any other shit we think might be useful. I don't think he'll be buried yet."

"Appreciate it, man."

"I'll keep you updated. I'll be calling the boys in Quebec unofficially, of course. I do speak a bit of French." I could only think he could speak not much more than a bit of English. He rang off.

I didn't know what to say. The news took me aback. It quite put me off my all-bran. It didn't take much to do that, of course. I rushed downstairs to talk to Red. His door was locked. I didn't want to disturb the two of them. But I didn't want to hear any more about Dr. Pimple Popper from Rita. I went outside to have a cig. Rita was very much against me smoking and I suppose I was. I had to hide my cigs in a plastic bag. They were stashed in a bird box in the garden. It was difficult for me to get to them and that apparently was part of the solution.

Red appeared with Jen about an hour later. He could tell that something was up. I was pacing around the kitchen.

"Something happen boss?" he said.

"Eric Horsfall was killed in a motor vehicle accident last night."

"On the second day, he was raised from the dead," Red replied.

It sounded sort of biblical. Not what I would have expected from Red. Then again, he was well read.

"It was just outside Montreal. Last night. And it seems as if it was him."

"So boss, who the fuck committed suicide the other night?"

"Good question. And apparently, this fella had been in Montreal for at least a couple of months."

You could almost see the wheels turning in Red's brain.

"If that's the case, who sent the threatening letters? They were posted in Calgary."

"Exactly," I replied.

"This is where we apply Occam's razor, Sid."

"Red, what the fuck do we want to use a razor for?"

Jen started laughing. I didn't see the funny side of this at all.

"Occam's razor essentially means that the simplest explanation is usually the correct one. It comes from an English friar about 700 years ago. We just covered it in philosophy," Jen said. "It's called Occam's razor." That was good, but I doubt I would need it in Trivia.

I could get quite defensive about this sort of stuff. Why not just say the simplest bloody explanation? I could be more than sensitive about my limited education.

"And the simplest explanation is?" I said.

"I think there are two issues here," said Red. "Unless this fella Horsfall had an accomplice here, he didn't send those letters. But more than that. Why would someone pretend to be Horsfall? And why would he kill Boudin if he ostensibly did not know him? And it begs another question. Did this man in Calgary actually commit suicide, or was it murder?" Red was quick to think this through. This Remington razor stuff seemed to work.

"The police obviously thought it was a suicide," said Jen.

"With all due respect, what the police think usually means Jack Shit in these cases," I replied.

"So, where do we go from here?" said Jen.

I liked the 'we' bit there. Talking like a team member.

"Let's get changed and pop into the Deer's Head cafe on Edmonton Trail. Have a good hot coffee and come up with some ideas. What do you think, Sid?"

"I like that suggestion, Jen," I replied.

I knew Rita would still be talking about Dr. Pimple Popper. But let me halt the narrative for a moment. You might think I'm unduly hard on Rita. Perhaps I am, but in reality, she is a fantastic bird. She ticks all the boxes as far as I am concerned. And she is capable of taking the piss out of me royally. Believe me, I have more faults than she does. If she reads this, she'll probably tell me to fuck off and throw a cushion at me. Then she'll remind me of all my faults and we'll laugh our heads off.

It only took five minutes to get to the Deer's Head cafe on Edmonton Trail. Doesn't look much from the outside but best breakfast deal in Calgary bar none. This time, we only wanted coffee. We did not include Jen. She had green tea.

Red started off the conversation.

"It seems obvious to me that the guy who committed suicide did not kill Boudin."

"Why's that?" said Jen.

"Several reasons. As I have already said, the killer could not have made it from the stage to the balcony in a couple of sessions. There simply had to be two guys. The question is which one was found dead?"

"The suicide surely was Bergman or someone going by that name. The guy who killed Boudin," I said. "Why would the other guy commit suicide?"

"We can't be sure of that. There's no evidence one way or another."

"Red, I have the feeling you think Bergman or whoever it was didn't commit suicide," I said.

"I don't. I think we are being led to believe that it was the balcony guy. I think this is a classic case of misdirection. But he wasn't Horsfall, and he didn't do the killing. Why would he commit suicide?"

"Perhaps he was murdered," said Jen.

This was met with silence. We all looked at each other, but we couldn't rule it out. I changed the subject.

"Of course, if the guy on the balcony was still alive," I said. "The question is, where is he now?"

"As I have said, I don't think he's alive," said Red. "If he turns up in the next few days, I'll admit I'm wrong."

"So, we either have to find the balcony man or, at the very least, find out who he was. Perhaps Louie can help us out on that one. He might be able to provide a positive ID on the suicide. We know for sure that whoever died was not Horsfall."

"I know this is completely speculative," said Red, "and I have no proof at all, but perhaps someone paid Bergman to murder Boudin. I can't think of too many suspects. I agree with Jen."

"And that someone is?" I replied.

The one person who has to come to mind is Marie. Who else had anything to gain? Going out on a complete limb. Perhaps she was having an affair with Horgan."

"That's hardly going out on a limb," I said.

"She was involved in an affair with Horgan, and they combined to snuff Boudin out. It certainly would not be the first time this had happened. If that was the case, how did they do it and why?"

"So, they could live happily ever after on the proceeds of his life insurance," I said. "It might motivate anyone, including me." I smiled as if it were a joke, but I'm not sure it was.

"Money can be a great motivator," Jen said, "but we have to find out how much the Life Insurance was worth."

"I bet Louie will be able to help us out with that. I'll call him later this morning."

"He usually can find anything out, boss," Red replied.

"Look team, there are a lot of questions to be asked," I said. "They say good detective work is just hard work. I think Red's ideas are interesting and take us in a whole new direction, but we have to get the evidence to back this up and keep Louie involved." I was trying to tell the team not to jump to any easy conclusions. Better if we proved ourselves wrong than have somebody else do it for us.

That was my idea of a rallying cry. I'm not sure it was needed. Red and Jen set off to surveil the warehouse. It was just a gut feeling, but I thought this was the day things would start to happen. Was this insight or just the years of being involved in these sorts of cases?

I went home to Rita. She told me she had taken all the cheques from Boudin to the bank. That was very efficient, but I wondered if she could get copies of them. I had a hunch, but I had to get those cheques.

I spent much of the rest of the morning answering some of the cell phone messages that had come in. I was a bit of a procrastinator. I had 28 messages. Several were from credit card companies telling me my card had been compromised. I didn't own any of the cards. One from the Canadian Revenue Agency demanding payment. If I didn't pay, I would be up shit creek. They didn't put it that way, but the message was obvious.

I eventually received a message from Jen. The occupants of the warehouse were apparently there. They would wait until Marie and Horgan left and then the field would be clear for us to have a look-see a few hours later. Then Jen said there was a really big surprise coming, but she would tell me later. I heard Red laughing in the background. What the fuck were they up to?

The first big break in the case came just after lunch. Louie called me. I'd never heard him breathless before. He was almost incoherent, slipping back into his native tongue.

"Louie, for fucks sake man, calm down, take a deep breath."

There was a moment's silence.

"Sid, we found the balcony guy."

"So, who the fuck was he?" I asked.

"He gave a statement to the cops. Read about the case in the newspaper."

"And?"

"His real name was Leonard Parr. Did a bit of acting with community theatre, murder mysteries. That sort of thing. Presently unemployed."

"What did he say?" I said.

"Mentioned that some guy called Horsfall asked him to do a gig at the theatre"

"Have any record?"

"One of the presidents of a community theatre group we talked to said he should have been indicted long ago for bad acting, but apart from that, he seemed to be harmless."

"I get the picture, Louie," I said. "It probably went down this way. Look, buddy, we've got a job for you. We want you to pretend to be this guy, Horsfall. It pays well. Nothing criminal about it. Just give us a quick yes or no. Oh, and the last guy to do this got a small part in a movie. How could a struggling actor say no?"

"He was living in his mother's basement for a few months. It seems as if he had come into a bit of money, but she didn't know where it was from," said Louie. "She said that he had mentioned doing the balcony job. He was still wearing the jacket with the emblem on when he came in. We didn't detain him. He's probably playing video games in his basement right now.

"Anything else worth noting?"

"Yes, she said that he had polio as a kid and limped a bit. Probably not important."

"I don't know about that," I said. "Some of the smallest clues can be the most important."

"I'll keep in touch," Louie said. "We'll see if the boys will reopen the case, but I wouldn't hold my breath. The big question is, where the fuck is Bergman. We think he's dead but he might be alive."?"

With that, he rang off. He was always apt to do that. No thanks for calling, no goodbyes, no see you. That was just the way Louie was.

It was only ten minutes later that Red called. Both Marie and Horgan had left for the day, or so they thought. The warehouse was likely to be unoccupied that night. They would be back home in about twenty minutes. I told them I had some really interesting news for them. When they asked what, I told them it could wait until they got back. Two could play at that game.

We all sat around the kitchen table drinking hot chocolate. The temperature had fallen like a rock. It was going to be minus 10 tonight. Rita had thought that hot chocolate would hit the spot, and she was right. I had only taken a few sips when I realized my cigs would be completely frozen. I wondered if I could eventually microwave them back to life.

Jen and Red arrived about half an hour later and they sat there grinning like Cheshire cats. They obviously had something significant to say.

"O. K," I said. "Let's have it. What's the big news?"

"Should I tell him or should you, Red?" said Jen.

"I think it should be you."

"Well, Red gave me a big surprise this afternoon."

"He paid for a round of drinks," I said.

Rita gave me a punch to the arm.

"Red got down on one knee in the bus and proposed."

"Fuck, you didn't say yes, did you?"

There was another punch to the same arm. I was going to have quite a bruise.

"Well, I considered it for a few seconds."

She was right, I thought. Don't let them see that you're too anxious.

"And then I said yes."

I picked up my cup of hot chocolate and proposed a toast to the couple. I was so happy for them. It had not been that long since they first met. Jen's previous boyfriend had a bit of a temper and was roughing her up a bit in a convenience store. Red was working part-time there. When he saw what was happening, he told the guy to get his arse out of the store and leave her alone. He was five foot six. He had no choice. And that was the beginning of things. Since she went into that store three or four times a week, they would meet quite frequently. She ditched her boyfriend and within weeks, Red had his boots under the bed. I remembered thinking this was a marriage made in 7-11 or a marriage of convenience..

Rita was into this a bit more than I was. At least, it stopped her talking about Dr. Pimple Popper. When, where, the best man, that sort of thing. Can I have a look at the ring? It went on and on. It was a girl......sorry woman thing.

About an hour later, I realized I had not told them my news. I felt a bit of a prick about that.

"So, folks, I got a call from Louie just after lunch. He had certainly done his job. The balcony guy was a bloke called Leonard Parr, an out-of-work actor. Apparently, he'd do anything for a buck."

"He was sure about that?" said Red.

"I don't think he would have called me otherwise."

"Anything else about him"?

"Nothing really........Oh, his mother said that he had a slight limp. Polio as a kid," I replied.

"Who asked him to do it?" I replied.

"Said he really couldn't provide an identity. It was pretty much done over the phone. It was a male but that hardly helps, does it?

Sounds plausible," I replied. "Anyway, let me change the subject for a moment. This is serious. If you're getting married, Red, you won't have any money unless you marry into it," I said.

I thought I was being funny. It was tactless. The third punch hurt the most. Red and Jen thought the whole thing was very funny.

"On second thoughts, if that's married life, I'm having second thoughts," Red said. I bruise easily.

We all laughed, but he missed the obvious point that I and Rita were not married. Perhaps it was a nudge in the wrong direction.

"Let's get back to business," said Red. "Where does this get us?"

"Look Red," I said. "We know Horsfall was not Horsfall And we also know that the man who committed suicide was somebody else. The problem is that we were led to believe that he was Horsfall. The big issue is why."

"The bigger issue is who the suicide victim was. We'd have to say Bergman. But......."

"But. Why do you say that Red?" said Jen.

"Doesn't quite make sense to me. A guilty conscience for killing someone. Come, come."

"Good point," suggested Jen. "But criminals are....... unpredictable. You're suggesting murder."

"Perhaps tonight will give us some insights. What time do you think we should go in there, Sid?" asked Red.

"Certainly, after midnight. A patrol car goes around there at about 11.30 every night. We're going to have to be careful. It won't be easy in this weather. We can't have any accidents."

"Meaning?" Said Red.

"We can't be arrested for burglary or worse, have a death by misadventure.".

"Fair enough," said Red. "What I would suggest is that Jen goes up first with a rope and then I get hauled up. Then I go through the skylight and do a basic search of the premises. We can't see any of the entrances front or back, so we can't see if anybody is coming in. Don't want any nasty surprises."

"One thing I don't want is evidence that we've been in there," I said. "Move nothing and for god's sake, don't take anything. Don't want Horgan or Marie getting suspicious. And I won't sit outside. No use in making it obvious that we are there. When you're through, I'll pick you up. And if you see any documents worth copying, use your cell phone."

"Sounds good," said Red. "Let's synchronize watches. Lift off at midnight."

"Synchronize watches," I said. "What the fuck is that? You've been watching 'Mission Impossible.'"

"Just pissing with you," said Red. Jen and I will get a bit of shut-eye for a few hours.

They disappeared hand in hand down the stairs.

"Shut eye?" I said to Rita. "He's just proposed to her. There will be fuck all shut eye."

"Arbuckle, you are a complete pig. What do you fancy for supper?"

15

FIVE MILLION DOLLARS

It had been snowing most of the night when we set off. That heavy wet stuff that eventually sticks and gets deep. It often plays havoc with the trees. There would be branches littered all over the place by the morning. The temperatures were later expected to plummet. They had already fallen a long way.

We took Deerfoot Trail on our way, but that was a mistake. There were cars in the ditch and the visibility was piss poor. It would have been better if I had put winter tires on. Almost as good if I had any tread on the tires I had. It was just a matter of economics. We drove slowly and tucked ourselves in behind a snowplow. But there were still dicks doing a hundred kilometres an hour down the road. Those guys usually survive. It's the people they hit who usually die.

We eventually reached the warehouse just after midnight. All seemed quiet. There were no tracks in the snow, so no cars had been there recently. We made sure to park some distance away. Any tracks we made would be obliterated in this wind. The guys got out and first made it to the bus. They climbed in and then I left. It was bloody cold, and I reminded myself that I would have to get the heater in my car repaired. It was going to be nice to snuggle up to Rita, assuming that she had forgiven me for the faux pas that afternoon.

It had been decided that once they were up on the roof, Jen would call me on her cell phone. I sat there until 12.30 AM watching re-runs of the Calgary Flames' only Stanley Cup win. Rita was messing about on her computer, looking for appropriate wedding gifts for the couple. A bit premature, but that's women for you. See, I got it right this time.

Jen called just after 1.00 AM. Red was in the warehouse. He had slipped the last few feet down to the warehouse floor and sprained his ankle. Probably good enough for a WCB claim but it apparently did not affect him too much. Red was not the sort to complain. He had disappeared into the warehouse for about twenty minutes. When he reappeared, he had a few items that he had stuffed into a bag, and he sent them up on a rope to Jen. So much for my instructions. She was so exposed up there. Her teeth were chattering when she called me.

Red then did a recce of the office. He looked through files and documents on the desk. There was something on the floor that he noticed and he picked it up. He then took a special interest in the two cabinets. He was using a torch, so it was very difficult for Jen to see what he was doing exactly.

Communications were kept to a minimum. Jen was wondering about how long she could survive up there when the situation changed dramatically. Red suddenly darted into one of the cabinets and turned off the torch at the same time. Seconds later, a figure emerged and turned on the desk lamp. It was still very dim in there, so it was very difficult to see who it was. The person was wearing a huge black anorak and snow boots and shades. It could have been anyone. She wondered if it could be a security guard, but ruled that out when the person opened the filing cabinet and took out some documents. It might have amounted to nothing, but there was a pool of water under the skylight, and it was noticed. At the same time, the cabinet swung open a few inches. The person walked over to the pool of water and looked up at the skylight. By this time, Jen had ducked away, so she wasn't seen. She thought that the person had gone into the warehouse and came back with a mop. The next time she looked, the floor was being mopped. Hopefully, whoever it was assumed that the roof was leaking and nothing more. That might have been it, but the person noted that the cabinet door had swung open and went across to the cabinet. Red was going to be discovered, and yet somehow he wasn't. The figure looked inside and closed the door. Where was Red? Fortunately, whoever it was didn't think to lock the cabinet door. That would have trapped Red. And then it was all over. The figure left, turning off the desk lamp. Red waited about ten minutes and then shone the flashlight to show that he was ready to leave. He climbed up the rope and they took shelter in the bus, which must have been like an icebox.

Jen called me and said they needed to get picked up. I went outside to my car. This was not an all-weather car. In fact, tonight it was a no-weather car. It simply wouldn't start. I quickly called Uber, and they promised to send a car right away. They didn't say they were going to send a Mini Cooper. I wasn't in any position to argue. We went the back way to the warehouse, avoiding the highways. There was nothing on the roads other than eighteen inches of snow, but somehow we got there and rescued the shivering duo. After we got home, I gave the driver a big tip. So, it was only twenty-five percent, but that's a big tip for me.

It was Jen who was suffering the most. We got her inside and Red got her into a hot shower. Rita came away from her computer long enough to ask me what was wrong with Jen. I told her that Jen was frigid, and Red had taken her downstairs to do something about it. As usual, I had butchered the English language, but she knew what I meant. Time for more hot chocolate.

Red had put his bag down on the way in. There didn't seem to be much in it. I was tempted to have a look-see but resisted the urge to do so. A few moments later, Jen appeared.

"Feeling better?" I said.

"I think my core temperature is recovering," she said

"How's Red?"

"He got the better of the deal. The warehouse is heated by a large furnace, so he had no problems with the cold."

"Where is he now?"

"He's downstairs. He's just downloading some photos he took."

"You were nearly caught," I said. "Any idea who it was?".

"That's right. Red was nearly caught. Don't know who it was. Could have been anyone. Could have been male. Could have been female. Could have been someone looking for money."

"You didn't see this person entering the warehouse?'"

"Not from the skylight. You can't see either the front or back entrance. But we saw the car tracks. The snow was already blowing over them when we got down off the roof. They'll be covered by now."

Red appeared up the stairs. It looked as if he'd shared the shower with Jen. That might have been a good idea for Rita and me, but it would have been a tight and probably impossible squeeze.

"No need to tell me about what happened in the warehouse," I said. "Jen told me all about it."

"Did she tell you I almost got caught?"

"She did."

"How come whoever it was didn't see you in the cabinet?"

"I slipped behind the mirror. It was very easy. Didn't take more than a couple of seconds."

"I've already given Sid a rundown of what happened," said Jen. "I think the important issue is what did you find Red and what relevance does it have to the case?"

"I couldn't have put it better myself," I said. "So, let's have a look at what we've got."

Red dropped a photograph on the table. It was a picture of a leather jacket with a tiger emblem on the back and a scarf. It looked identical to the one worn by Bergman. He had found it in Horgan's locker.

"So, two jackets suggest doubling. You agree Red."

"It would appear so."

"I'm glad that you didn't move the jacket," I said. "That would have been tampering with evidence. That's a bit of a no-no."

There was a pregnant pause. There was a knowing glance between Red and Jen.

"OK. I admit it. I took it away, but Jen made me put it back," said Red.

"Good thinking girl...I mean, young lady," I said.

"So Red, what do you think this all means?" I said.

"It's clear now that Horgan was Bergman," he said. "He must have killed Boudin. The question was whether Marie knew about this. I think she did."

"How can you be so sure?" I said.

"She was the one who fingered Horsfall as the likely killer. And she must have known that Bergman was Horgan. Hell, she was having an affair with him. How could she not recognize him in the theatre?"

"And she picked Horgan out of the crowd," I said.

"Good point."

"I'm surprised that they let that Parr guy get away with the other jacket. That was careless, to say the least. He might have been living on borrowed time. Another suicide?"

"Not necessarily. They could have just asked for it back. Let's not jump to conclusions," said Jen.

"Anything else?" I asked.

"I found these two placards in the warehouse," said Red. "Recognize them, Sid?"

"I recognize one of them," I said. "The last will and testament signed by Pierre Boudin. And this one is stained with blood. We should get Louie to get this tested. I assume it's Boudin's blood. He must have been wearing it when he was stabbed."

"I think the reason there were two is quite obvious."

"Not to me, it isn't," I replied.

"There'd have to be two of them. One for Boudin, the blood-stained one, and one for the Boudin double, who had to have gone in the cabinet on the right. That's why we found two."

"Fuck, I'd completely forgotten about that. Jesus, we have somebody else to identify. This is getting too bleeding complicated for me."

"Sooner or later, we will have to work it all out," said Red.

"No wonder the police wanted to close this case so quickly. I can't blame them. Anything else you found in there?" I asked.

"Nothing of substance, but some oddities that I noticed behind Marie's desk. It looked like a vial of blood. Course, I didn't open it and it could have been a stage effect," Red said.

"Anything else? "

"Yes, there is. Exhibit one. It was an e-mail ticket and schedule for Mr. Stephen Horgan. It was a one-way ticket to Johannesburg paid for by Marie."

Red plonked a copy down on the table

"What the fuck is Horgan doing flying to South Africa?" I said. "And when?".

Jen looked at the ticket.

"In four days' time," she said. "He should be packing by now."

A woman's comment. They tend to pack days early. If I go anywhere, I pack about an hour before I leave. A couple of shirts, a sweater, a pair of pants, and six pairs of underpants. I mean you can never be too careful. Oh, and a bottle of mouthwash, but they usually confiscate that.

"We can speculate what that is all about later. Anything else of interest?" I said.

"I left the most interesting thing to the last," said Red. "A copy of Boudin's Life Insurance......the one Marie didn't know about."

"Do you have a copy?" I said.

"Just didn't have time to copy it," he said.

"So how much was it for?" said Jen.

"A cool five million dollars. Marie took the policy out on her husband about three months ago. And she didn't remember doing it. I'd call that selective amnesia."

"So, she had a lot to gain from his death. Five million dollars of gain," I added.

"More than enough for a motive," said Jen.

"I might consider it for a lot less," I replied.

"There was one other thing that I found. It was on the floor of the warehouse. Just a post-it note saying 'I love you,' Marie."

At that point, Rita had walked in.

"How sweet," she said. "Romance isn't completely dead."

"Well, my bloody coffee cup is," I replied. I winked at her. She took the hint and buggered off into the kitchen.

"Anything else?" said Jen.

"Not really," said Red.

"You guys did well. I think we can put two and two together and make four."

"Horgan and Marie were heavily involved, and she had her husband killed for the money," said Red.

"The bitch," said Jen.

Now I never considered Jen to have a potty mouth. She was quite irate.

"That bitch killed her husband for his life insurance," she continued. "Then she planned to run away with the handyman. It's obvious."

"It would certainly seem so," I said. "Nothing unusual about this sort of thing. It should be the first thing you would think of in these cases. I've seen quite a few of them. It wouldn't happen to me, of course. My policy only covers burial costs. Come to think of it, it's probably delinquent by now."

"It all seems straightforward," said Red, but can we prove it? "It's all circumstantial evidence to me. Sometimes the obvious is not that obvious in these cases."

"I agree," said Jen. "Let's assume the obvious is true. I mean, if we accuse them, they would just deny, deny, deny. But you should call Louie about this. There is some interesting information here. He should be able to help one way or another."

"Oh, I will call him, for sure," I said.

"I think we can guess what's happened here," said Jen. "The issue is, what do we do now?"

"That's for Sid to decide, Jen, but I tell you one thing. We just can't let Horgan escape. He'll be out of the country in four days,"

"We'll find a way to stop him," I said.

"And if we don't? Sid, do we have an extradition treaty with South Africa?"

"Not sure. I'll check it out, but I don't think we need to do anything dramatic, at least for the next little while. We could easily fuck this up. I think we need a bit more information. We continue to surveil tomorrow....agree. I think we should see Marie again hopefully and have Louie with us. Put the pressure on big time. Let her dig a bigger hole for herself. Let the police realize they fucked up."

"That's the way to do it," said Red. "If you tell the police they fucked up, they'll dig their heels in."

"A nice psychological principle in there somewhere," said Jen.

"I think there's something else we could do," I said.

"What's that?" said Jen.

"You never know. We might find Horgan's apartment door ajar, if you know what I mean? I'm sure a visit to his apartment could be very enlightening. People can be very careless with their doors."

"You're not suggesting breaking in, are you?"

"Did I say that?" I winked at Red. "Think we're fucking criminals?" Everyone laughed.

At that moment, Rita appeared again. She mentioned that tonight would be a celebration of Red and Jen's engagement. She had prepared a steak dinner for everybody. What a sweetie she was, but she had quite forgotten that Jen was a vegetarian.

When dinner was served, I surreptitiously gobbled down Jen's meat even though it was hardly on my healthy heart diet. Rita was none the wiser. Still, in a celebratory mood, she suggested going down to the casino to play a few slots. Not a highlight for me, but everyone else seemed in the mood. I wouldn't normally have mentioned this, but as they wandered around inserting coins, we came across a slot machine called the Illusionists. It was too good to miss, and Red inserted a dollar coin. Would you believe it? Lights started flashing, bells started ringing, and a message flashed up. He had won three hundred and fifty-seven bucks. Was this an omen for the future?

"You lucky bastard," I said. "Beginner's luck that."

"How wonderful," said Rita. "You know, that'll buy a nice wedding ring for Jen."

"Nah," I said. "That will provide a nice down payment on a new car. You have to be sensible these days."

I was taking the piss, and I half expected another punch to my arm, but what I got was something that I couldn't have expected.

"You mean you wouldn't buy a nice ring for me," she said.

My blood turned to ice. I'd sort of thought about this, but had been repressing the thought for a few weeks. I had been burned in matrimony a few times. Was she proposing? Holy fuck, I was going to have to make a few decisions very shortly.

16

PIZZA FOR TWO

I was up early the following morning. The wind had died down, and the sun had appeared. It would do little to warm things up. Minus 10 centigrade was not extreme, but it was not exactly comfortable, especially when it was damp. But It was going to be a brief episode of winter. There was a Chinook forecast for the weekend. The locals called it a snow eater, and it usually lived up to its name. We could expect the temperatures to get back above freezing, but it probably wouldn't last long. My cigs were probably encased in a block of ice by now.

I called Louie before eight and left a message that we should meet that morning. I was due to drop off Rita at her psychologist. Nothing to worry about. Just a few emotional problems that she had had since a tough childhood. I thought she just wanted someone to talk to, and I felt guilty that it wasn't me.

I arranged to meet Louie at ten thirty at one of those fancy, overpriced latte places. But since it wasn't me who would pay ten dollars for a latte and a croissant, I wasn't that bothered. Louie was fascinated by what I had to report, but he agreed everything was circumstantial, though not insignificant. He agreed that Marie's selective amnesia for the life insurance was more than suspicious. But she would probably say she had forgotten when questioned in court and the judge or jury would believe her.

Louie said that he was free in the late afternoon and would call Marie to insist on a meeting. I also talked about the placard with the blood on it. I asked him if it was possible to see if we could get a blood match. Louie had contacts. He said it would take a couple of hours. So, I gave it to him. He said he would contact me later to confirm the meeting with Marie. As usual, he was up and away and forgot to pay the bill. I wouldn't come to this place again. You needed a line of credit to pay the bill.

When Rita and I got home, Red and Jen had already left to surveil the warehouse. They parked in a place where they could only see the front door, but it would probably be good enough. They were certainly dressed for the occasion and had taken a handful of those hand and foot warmers from my closet. You know those things that come in a packet. You break them and a chemical reaction produces warmth. They had also taken a flask of hot coffee. The bus was probably encased in ice, so it was very difficult to see in and probably not that easy to see out.

They left a message just after lunch to say both Marie and Horgan were in the building. They also mentioned that a pizza courier carrying what looked to be a large pizza had approached the front door and had been let in. He was wearing some sort of uniform, but they couldn't identify it.

They thought they might order a pizza from him when he came out. The problem was that they never saw him come out. Very strange. He could have come out through the back entrance, I suppose, but that didn't seem likely. They continued to watch, but that incident made little sense. They assumed in the end that they had just missed him. And that was the end of any activity for a few hours. But they noticed the furnace seemed to be working at maximum, given the billowing white smoke from the roof. What the hell were they burning in there? It sure as hell wasn't time for a new pope.

Louie had not been able to contact Marie, but it didn't matter to Louie. He would just turn up and bullshit his way in. Asking to search the warehouse would be a bit of a problem because he didn't have a search warrant. But if she refused, it would just add to the mounting suspicions. He could always get one. We arrived at 4.30 and she did let us in. She had already met Louie, but when she saw us, she bluntly inquired why we were there. I told you Louie could bull shit. He said we had been co-opted as special assistants to the case. It was a bit like Westerns. We had been sworn in as deputies. Louie came straight to the point.

"Marie, I'm a bit concerned about the Life Insurance. You denied to the police that you were aware of it."

"I had quite forgotten about it. You must understand that I was an emotional wreck when you first talked to me."

"That's very surprising," said Louie. "It was you who took out the insurance....I believe it was for 5 million dollars...and you were paying the premiums."

"I leave that sort of thing to my accountant. He pays all the bills."

Unless you're paying Lou Diamond, I thought. I said nothing.

"And the beneficiary of the Life Insurance?" Louie said.

"Since you seem to know everything else, I suspect you know very well. You know it would be me and me alone."

At that point, we all seemed to hear something bang at the back of the warehouse. We all looked in that direction and then at each other.

"That sounded like the rear entrance door banging," Marie said. "Excuse me while I secure the door."

If the door had been open, it had done little to lower the temperature in there. A warm breeze wafted in. from the furnace room. It was roasting. We were all feeling a little uncomfortable.

"What you think?" said Louie.

"I think she is a pretty smooth customer," I said. "She'll have an answer for everything.'

We heard the back door slam, and she reappeared a few seconds later.

"Do you have any more questions, inspector?"

Louie was not, in fact, an inspector, and I doubt that he ever would be. He just didn't fit the template. But he was not going to correct her.

"I do. So just relax for a few minutes and we can get this over rather quickly."

"I know that I'm not under any caution, so I know I don't have to answer your questions, but I will. But be quick. I am very busy wrapping up my husband's affairs." Thank god this was not followed up with the dry tears we'd seen previously.

"Tell me about Stephen Horgan. There have been rumours you had been romantically involved with him."

"That's absurd." She feigned a laugh. "I can't imagine why anyone would say such a thing. Steven and I were such good friends. I think the word is platonic, inspector."

"I was hoping to speak to Steven today," said Louie. "Any idea where he could be?"

"Look, I'll be honest with you," she said.

This could be a first for the day, I thought to myself.

"Stephen and I had a bit of a bust-up this morning. He got quite emotional. His behavior was quite unacceptable. I asked him to leave."

"About what?" I said.

"Let's say artistic issues." I wonder what the fuck that meant, but I didn't pursue the issue.

"And he up and left?"

"He did, indeed, with a month's payout. I think under the circumstance I was being generous."

"Where is he now?"

"I have no idea. He said he was leaving this shitty province and not soon enough."

That was fighting talk designed, I'm sure, to completely piss both of us off.

"Had he any plans to leave the province before this?" Louie asked.

"Not that I'm aware of. Perhaps he planned to, in the future. Men... well you never know."

She was smooth. We both knew she was lying her arse off.

"Did he leave a forwarding address?" I said.

"I have his address somewhere. I'll phone it into you."

"Perhaps you can tell me what the argument was about and be specific," Louie said.

"I know I'm not obligated, but I will tell you. Stephen had aspirations to be the next great illusionist.....the next Boudin if you like. I know he'd been trying to cozy up to me. Some people had observed it. He probably thought he could get the rights to Boudin's illusions through me. I was emotionally broken. I didn't realize what was going on. Perhaps I needed a shoulder to cry on. It seems I chose the wrong shoulder. Why do men always have an agenda?"

Not only attacking my province, but she was attacking my gender. She was right. Most men do have an agenda. Just not the one she'd be comfortable with. We're pretty simple creatures.

"You know, inspector, some men pray on us. We are like putty in their hands. They......."

For fuck's sake, Louie, I thought. Get her to stop. This is painful. This woman would have done well in a Victorian melodrama or a Hallmark card.

"Yes, yes, I see," said Louie. "Well, if he should contact you, let him know that we want to talk to him.'

"So that's it?" she said.

"Not quite," said Louie. "I hope you don't mind if I look around."

"Would it make any difference if I did mind?"

"I don't suppose it would, my dear," he said.

'My dear.' And they thought I was politically incorrect. But Louie could get away with it. I usually couldn't.

"I'll just look in the warehouse. Just a quick look-see. Doubt there's anything to see."

For the first time, her composure seemed to wane. She was hiding something; we knew she was hiding something, and we knew she knew we knew she was hiding something. It was just a game.

"Before I do anything else," said Louie, I was looking at the shelf behind you. Are those vials of blood?"

She didn't realize that Louie didn't have his glasses on and couldn't possibly have seen them. She turned to the shelf and removed one of the vials.

"They are, indeed, vials of blood, inspector. One thing you may not have known about the great Boudin was that realism was everything. Stage blood is notoriously fake. It looks nothing like the real thing. He used this in some of his illusions. It would sometimes freak the audience out." Hell, it would probably freak me out.

"I'm not surprised," said Louie. "Lot of blood phobias out there. Anyway, I'll just take a look at the warehouse. It shouldn't take long."

In fact, it shouldn't have taken long. Because he knew exactly what he was looking for. While he was away, I indulged in a more casual conversation with Marie. I knew she wouldn't answer any pointed questions.

"This has all been very difficult for you," I said. "What is going to happen now?"

"It's difficult to say," she said. "I am thinking of moving all the equipment down to Medicine Hat. My brother-in-law will be here later today to discuss storage." Perhaps she meant Montmartre. I prevented myself from laughing, but only just.

"Your brother-in-law. Boudin had a brother?".

"Technically no. He had a stepbrother. They weren't very close at all. They were just very different temperaments."

"What does he do for a living?"

"IT, I think. That sort of thing. He's a whiz with computers."

"Did he attend the cremation?" I asked.

"As a matter of fact, he did not. You know Mr. Diamond; I would have made you a coffee, but we're fresh out."

She obviously wanted to change the subject

"And fresh out of pizza as well."

"You have incredible olfaction," she said.

I did? What the fuck was olfaction?

"Olfaction?" I looked at her quizzically.

"It's how you smell," she said. I wasn't sure whether this was a personal comment. I assumed it wasn't.

''I could detect the aroma of pizza.''

"That's right. We had a pizza earlier."

"Smells good. Where do you get it?"

"Some small joint near Chinook. Don't remember the name."

I realized that at this point Red had not asked a question. He didn't need to. He would take all of this in, and he wouldn't miss a word.

Louie came back in a few minutes later. Probably wasted a bit of time smoking a cig. He was carrying the leather jacket and scarf that Red had so nearly absconded with the night before.

I half expected Marie to shit herself, metaphorically, of course. She didn't bat an eyelid.

"I found these clothes in Mr. Horgan's locker. Weren't these the clothes that the Bergman character was wearing? What the hell would they be doing in Horgan's locker?"?

I didn't think there was an answer to this, but there was.

"I thought I mentioned this to the police, but they didn't seem to be that interested."

"Mentioned what?" I asked.

"We found those clothes dumped on the stage right after the murder. The killer must have thrown them off. I know Mr. Horgan was keeping them just in case the police would want to examine them. I'm sure we'd mentioned it the last time we talked."

I'm sure they hadn't mentioned it. What she didn't realize was that she had given the balcony man the perfect alibi. Not that he really needed it now. How could he have appeared on the balcony wearing exactly the same clothes? Perhaps he did some one-stop shopping at Moore's on the way to the balcony.

"Well, that seems to be it, for now, said Louie. "Oh, there is one thing. I found this gold pendant in the warehouse. It was right by the furnace. Any ideas?"

"Let me have a look at it, inspector." Louie gave it to her. She quickly examined it. But only briefly.

"Of course, this is Stephen's. You can see the SH engraved on the front. He was always losing it. You can see the clasp is loose."

"If he comes back for it, you'll let us know," I said.

"I'm not sure he will," Marie answered. "I got the feeling he wouldn't be coming back. He was furious. He doesn't need the money or any reference."

With that, we left the warehouse. There was no doubt that Marie was one cool customer. She could lie and then cover up the lie in a nanosecond. But she, for now, was not the big issue. The issue was Stephen Horgan. Where was he and why had she bought him a ticket to South Africa? Before we left, we went to the back of the warehouse. There were some fresh footprints in the icy snow outside. I suppose the pizza man might have left that way. Horgan's motorbike was not there. It was time to drop into the Dog and Duck to review the situation. Jen would be waiting for us there.

When we got there, it was empty, apart from Jen. Just a bit too early for the supper time rush. Not that there was much of a rush these days. With social distancing, it had been, and continued to be, difficult for these establishments. Louie looked anxious as he sat down.

"We can't make any arrests right now", he said. "Not quite enough evidence to convince anybody, but I am worried about what happened to Horgan."

"Why would that be?" Jen said.

"Just a gut feeling."

"Based on what?" I asked.

"Based on a couple of things. First, he suddenly quits and wants out of the province. Perhaps it was done in a fit of spite. Who knows?

Second, I found something in the warehouse that made me feel very uncomfortable."

"What was that?" I asked.

"I found a pizza box with what appeared to be a garotte in it."

"Could it not have just been part of an illusion?" I asked. "There was plenty of bizarre shit in the warehouse."

"Of course, anything is possible," he said. "But why would it be in a pizza box?"

"Do you still have the box and garotte?'

"No, but I moved it to somewhere in there where it would not be easily found. Forensics may have to look at that."

"I don't know whether you know this, but there was a pizza delivered to the warehouse today. We don't know what happened to the delivery man," Jen said.

"I think we've still got a lot to do. And the first thing is to find Stephen Horgan and the sooner the better," I said.

"Do you want us to drive over to his apartment right now, Sid?" said Jen.

"I do. And if you find him, let me know as soon as possible."

"Thank you," said Louie. "I think his life could be in danger."

17

I'M MR. BATTY

It was great to have Louie involved again. He could add so much, and he did almost right away. We had arranged to meet at the working man's coffee house the next morning. No fancy lattes this time, in part because I thought I'd have to pay. When he arrived, I realized this was the serious Louie. No jokes, no pissing about.

He plonked himself down beside me. This was the off-duty version of Louie. He was wearing a t-shirt that said "Romania...that's my sort of mania". Someone might have thought it amusing. I couldn't imagine who.

"So, what gives, big fella?" I said.

"I got the results from the placard. It was Boudin's blood all right. No doubt about it.".

"It must have come from when he was stabbed," I said. "Anything else?"

"You know that e-mail confirmation for the trip to South Africa, I called the agent who released the ticket."

"And?"

"It was canceled yesterday, just after lunch."

"By whom?"

"One would have to think it was Marie. If she'd argued with Horgan, she could have done it out of spite, but there could be another reason."

"What's that?" I said.

"Rather not say for now. Don't like tempting providence, Sid."

"Don't tempt it, but let me know if you're right. I know you will."

"Any news of Horgan?" Louie asked.

"Jen and Red went down to his apartment last night," I said. "Waited there for three hours. Nothing. His belongings seemed to be still there, but no motorbike. When they went down to the warehouse, this morning it was not there either. Now, to be fair, who the fuck would ride a motorbike in this weather? But if that was the case, why was it not abandoned at the warehouse yesterday? Then a slice of luck. The guys were just leaving and had gone about fifty yards down the road when Jen spotted it. It appeared to have been thrown into the Auto Dump facility."

"You mean the place for old crapped out cars and bikes just down the road from the warehouse? You know it?"

"Exactly," I said. I didn't admit that was where I got my first car.

"Why would he dump it? I mean, it was a piece of crap, but it was still worth something."

"Louie, you said, 'Why would he dump it'. Somebody else could have dumped it," I replied.

"True. But for his health's sake, I hope not. Any other activity from the warehouse?"

"Not much. Somebody turned up in a black Merc with tinted windows. These guys drove fancy cars, almost certainly leased," I said.

"Any idea who it was?"

"Dunno. Nobody we know. Short arse. Bald as a coot."

"Probably flogging time-share condos in Canmore," said Louie with a laugh. He should have known. That was his first job in Canada. I could imagine his spiel. Have a big condom for you. Big enough for two. You want?

"Just a minute," I said. "Marie told me that some relative was coming in today. Who was it?"

"I think she said stepbrother or something."

"What I should do," said Louie, "is to go down to Horgan's apartment and use the old routine to root around. Remember?"

"Course, I remember," I said. "I'll go down there right away and see what we can find."

With that, he was up and away, but after a few feet, he stopped and turned around.

"Fifty should cover the coffee," he said. He deposited a fifty-dollar bill on the table. "That's for next time as well."

That was the Louie I remembered. He would have made somebody a good husband. He just didn't have the time. Then again, it was probably the reason he had the money to be so generous.

I immediately drove down to 17th Ave SE. We had to find Horgan. Perhaps it was a matter of life and death. When I got there, I could see that there was nobody in but there was a supervisor of the complex. I knocked on his door. An elderly manager answered the door.

"Excuse me," I said. "My name is Mervyn Batty, from the City of Calgary engineer's department. We are looking for a gas leak and we think it's coming from one of these apartments. There's no need to panic, but if we don't find it, we might have to evacuate. We suspect it's coming from that apartment over there." I pointed at Horgan's apartment.

"Not a problem," he said. "I'll let you in right away, Mr. Batty."

"Do you need my card?"

"No need," he replied. Of course, I didn't have one, but people never asked. A bit of psychology in that ruse.

It was a fairly spartan place, but it was very neat and tidy. There was a half-eaten bowl of cereal on the kitchen table. If he'd been back that day, he would certainly have cleaned that up. It certainly did not look as if he had left town. All his clothes seemed to be present and, more importantly, if he had left, he probably did so without his three pairs of shoes. When people leave on the spur of the moment, they usually take most of their shoes.

It was only when I took a closer look in his drawers that I really hit the jackpot. There was something odd about one of his sports socks. It was more than odd. It contained about two thousand dollars in cash. Now I not suggesting that he had stolen this. Even if he had, I would not have been particularly bothered. The fact was that people simply do not skip town, leaving a couple of grand in a sock.

That was not everything. When I lifted his shirts, there was a plastic bag sitting underneath. I opened it very slowly. It contained a knife. I could see that it was stained with blood. I was not about to touch that. None of my fingerprints could go on it. The police could take care of this. Had I found the murder weapon? It certainly looked like it. Of course, he could have been cutting up blood sausages, and the knife had accidentally fallen in underneath his shirt. No. I remembered that Remington Razor principle. The simplest explanation and all that stuff.

The next thing we had to do was to find the murderer. Finding the knife had only moved us so far. We knew who had killed Boudin now, but I'm sure we all felt there was something more to this story.

On the way out, I bumped into the supervisor. He asked me whether I'd found the gas leak. I told him I had. I said I would be sending a couple of guys down later. There was no need to add that they would probably be dressed as police officers.

Moments later, I called Louie with the news. He wasn't available, so I left a message. I then called Red. He said that Marie and the bald-headed stranger had just left in the swanky black car. He obviously couldn't say whether they would come back. There was one thing worrying me. If Marie felt the pressure, who was to say that she wouldn't make a run for it? Although I doubted whether a cheque had been written on the life insurance policy, these things were usually paid pretty quickly. If Horgan had done a runner, what was to stop her from doing the same? The problem was that I didn't actually think that Horgan had done that. I had a very bad feeling about his health.

Louie did eventually get back to me. He was intrigued by what I had to tell him. He still thought it might be some time before the police would react. There were going to be mass demonstrations against the Covid lockdown in the next couple of days and all police leave had been cancelled. It was very brave of the demonstrators. They might not die of Covid, but pneumonia was a distinct possibility if they were out there too long.

Louie was intrigued by the visitor to the warehouse and wondered if we had taken down the car registration. Red was a professional. Of course, he had. Louie said that he would find out who was driving the car and would get the information back to me pronto. Louie also thought it might be worthwhile doing a missing person's report on Horgan

I suggested that Red and Jen stop their surveillance and come back home, at least for the time being. I had some suspicions developing. Perhaps it was something in my paranoid makeup.

When they arrived home, Louie had just called me. The driver of the Merc seemed to be who we thought. His name was Luke Baldipp, and he was apparently Boudin's stepbrother. The car had been bought from Boudin a couple of weeks earlier. Not bad for somebody involved in IT. I was in the wrong profession.

Everything Marie had told me seemed to pan out. Was he here to help her out? If he was that helpful, why was he not at the cremation and the reception? He must have been busy repairing computers that day. One thing that puzzled me was why he had a different surname as Horton aka Boudin. There was probably a simple answer.

Louie also said that he would be visiting Horgan's apartment to have it locked down. Nobody would be allowed in. There was one interesting piece of news. He had called the travel advisor about the cancelled flight ticket. She said the person who had cancelled the ticket also enquired about the costs of two tickets to Canberra, Australia. It might mean something. It might mean nothing.

Early that evening, after the police had put out a missing person report on Horgan, they received a tip from an anonymous source. Some guy had called in and said that a man answering Horgan's description had been seen at a cheap motel in Canmore. He was acting suspiciously, but on what basis, God only knew. Still, I thought I would check it out. I asked Red and Jen to accompany me out to Canmore that evening. Since the chinook had blown in, the roads were clear. It would be a pleasant trip to Canmore, especially as we drove into the setting sun behind the mountains. The Sleepy Lodge Motel looked as if it had fallen asleep years ago. It was what you'd call budget lodging. A paint job would probably have made it worse. I mean, I would stay there. It was the sort of place that had cleanish beds and was a decent step up from those places you rent by the hour, I'm told.

When we got there, we went to the main desk and asked if a Stephen Horgan was staying there. They didn't know. He certainly hadn't registered as Horgan. No one had that week, but there was a Stephen in room 15, they said. He had come in from Calgary last night. He was on his own. I knocked on the door of room 15. Stephen opened the door. He was Chinese. I told him I was looking for Shirley and must have the wrong room.

When you have a missing person alert, you often get false reports. Some people seem to get a kick from phoning them in. But I wondered if this had been sent in to simply muddy the waters. In fact, it was to be the only report that we got that day.

I didn't think too much about it because it allowed me to take in some fine dining in Canmore. And there was a good choice. I know what you're thinking. Sidney Arbuckle wouldn't know the difference between one burger joint and the next, but I would. I enjoy fine dining. I got into haute cuisine years ago. My first wife was into that sort of stuff. It was the only thing I gained from that marriage that and a few pounds.

We slipped into a little Asian-based restaurant. It had only just opened after the Covid business. I won't tell you what I had because

I didn't remember and almost certainly would not have been able to pronounce it. It was a delightful evening, and we tried hard not to talk about work. But it was inevitable. Somehow we had managed to get a new contract for vetting job applicants for the new Covid Investigation team. This was a very lucrative contract, and it would be very time-consuming. If we were going to solve the Boudin case, we had better do it quickly. We decided that we would have another look inside the warehouse and further liaise with Louie. The one thing we had to avoid was Marie doing a runner.

18

CHROME DOME

Nine times out of ten, a hunch is just a hunch, and it goes nowhere. But once in a while, they hit the jackpot. I mean you are never particularly optimistic, but if it pays off you congratulate yourself on being the next best thing after Sherlock Holmes. One thing I should say is that you usually keep your hunches to yourself, and I didn't mention it to the team. Just after breakfast, I called the Pumphouse Theatre. They were in early that day. I asked if I could look at the auditorium. That would not be a problem, but it would be a problem if they had thoroughly cleaned the stage. They hadn't. The police had said that it was a crime scene and to leave it until further notice. They had. The case had been closed, but nobody had been good enough to tell the staff.

When I got there, they opened up the theatre and gave me free rein. I would be on my own for twenty minutes. Of course, some people would argue that you are never entirely on your own at the Pumphouse. There had been rumours of ghosts in there for years. People had reported hearing a piano playing. There is no piano in the Pumphouse. Or they would hear the sound of boot steps. Lights going on and off. You get the idea. That wouldn't phase me. I think it's all a load of bollocks. So, I wasn't looking over my shoulder when I inspected the stage.

The first thing I did was check how easy it would be to get to the stage to the balcony. I already knew that balcony man could not have gotten up there in a few seconds. I ran, albeit not very quickly, and it took about 30 seconds. Another nail in the coffin for the' balcony man did it' theory. But that was not why I was there. I went back down to the stage, took out a sharp knife, and started scraping. It only took about two minutes and I put the scrapings in a plastic bag and then made to leave the theatre. Shit, I thought I heard a piano playing.

Louie didn't have time to meet for more than a brief meeting. There had been a fatality on the LRT line in the northeast just by the zoo. He was part of the investigation. It could have been an accident. They usually weren't. It was an occupational hazard for the drivers. Some of them had seen two or three incidents, and I knew a few were being treated for PTSD.

I met Louie at the Zoo station. I handed over my little deposit, and he said he would have it processed within a couple of days. He had also questioned the contact at the travel agency. She said that the inquiry about Canberra had come from a male. She said she thought the call had come from a cell phone but could not identify the caller. It was something and it might eventually become part of the puzzle later. And then he asked me to do something that surprised me. He wanted someone from the team to go back into the warehouse and retrieve the pizza box and the garotte. He said that he had hidden the items behind the furnace. It was, of course, slightly illegal, but he was willing to take the consequences should there be any. I said that I would see if Red and Jen could do this that night. Louie said he'd had a hunch. He wouldn't tell me what it was. I understood perfectly. Oh, and the blood vials contained Boudin's blood. That supported Marie's story, but I wasn't betting on Marie's story. There was nothing simple about this case.

Since I had some free time, I thought I might as well drive down to the warehouse, but before I did so, I thought I would contact an associate from my police days. He was a big name in computers. I think he lectured at the local college.

I had been stationed for a year in Medicine Hat. I had moved there after my second marriage. So, not many happy memories of the place. I couldn't remember the guy's first name, but everybody responds to "Heh, buddy. It's Sid here." I called him.

"Who the fuck are you?" he said. Then there was the sound of laughing. "How goes it, Sid? Long time, no see ....you wanker."

A nice friendly welcome followed by the usual "You getting laid, still got any hair, need Viagra.'" That's just the way old guys greet each other these days.

"Piss off," I said. He laughed. We were already getting along famously." Look, Buddy", I said, "I wonder if you know anything about this fella Luke Baldipp. He apparently is into IT in the Hat."

"Oh, fuck you mean chrome dome? Weird fuck he is."

"What do you mean?'"

"An odd guy. Lives on an acreage just west of here. A bit of an isolate. A real short arse."

"Married?"

"You're shitting me. He doesn't have too many friends. I don't think he would know what to do with a woman if he found one. He probably has 'Sex for Dummies' on his shelf.

"You mean Dummies for Sex?"

"Probably." He laughed.

"Anything else?"

"Yeah, he's really neat and tidy. I think he's obsessive compulsive., admittedly not a professional diagnosis."

"Not a bad thing for someone in his profession," I said.

"This guy sure keeps himself scarce. I haven't seen him in months."

After that, we limited ourselves to idle chit-chat. I invited him to pop in to see me in Calgary for a drink.

"Do you ever come this way?" I said.

"Funny you mention that I'll be at a conference there in a couple of days. I'll give you a call."

I wondered if he'd call. If he did, I would have to remember his name in a hurry. I was on my way down to the warehouse when I received an urgent call from Louie. I had only just talked to him. He did not seem in a good mood.

"Bit of a fuck up here in department. I'm pissed."

"What is it?' I said.

"We received a credible warning a couple of days ago detailing a threat of violence against Marie. Nobody told me until right now. Fuck them!!"

"Louie," I said. "Probably a crank call. We used to get them all the time."

"Crank call Bullshit. It came from Boudin's cell phone. It was made in Calgary. Gotta go, buddy."

What the fuck was going on here? Any thoughts would have to wait until I could talk to the team

When I got down to the warehouse, the Merc was sitting outside, but I did not immediately see Marie's car. It was unusual not to see it. When I asked the guys about it, they said they hadn't seen it all morning. This was a first. Nothing was said, but I'm sure we were all wondering whether Marie had done a runner as we had all feared. I didn't say anything but immediately contacted a friend of mine at customs and immigration. They had no record that she had left the country, at least not using her own passport. So where was she? She could have been having a manicure for all we knew. But it didn't answer the question of why Baldipp was there on his own. She could have given him a key, but what was he doing in there? It was time to have a chat with Mr. Chrome Dome.

When I buzzed at the door, he appeared to be on his way out. But after we introduced ourselves, he appeared to be on his way back. He was quite polite. He could have told us to piss off, but he escorted us into the office area. We told him we were looking to interview Marie. In fact, we were looking to interview him. As we sat down, his cell phone rang. He put it down without answering it.

"Coffee, sir?"

"Not for me," I said.

"Mind if I pour myself one?"

"No problem," we said in unison.

"What can I do for you?"

"Marie was telling me that you had come over from Medicine Hat to help."

"That's right. I know she's been very upset. I'd do anything to help out. Most of Boudin's family are gone. Several died with Covid, I think. His mother and I believe there was an aunt."

This Boudin thing was something else. That was his stepbrother talking. I would have called him Doug, his real name.

"How long have you been in Calgary?"

Baldipp looked at his watch.

"Give or take a few minutes. I would say about sixteen hours."

"When are you going back to Medicine Hat?"

"Possibly today. Probably tomorrow. I don't think Marie will need any more help."

"How did you get on with Doug?"

"Look, I don't want to kick a man when he is down, but I found him to be s-s-upers-c-c- ilious."

"Shit, I always had trouble with that word. I couldn't pronounce it and I couldn't tell you what it meant."

"Meaning?"

"He was a bit of an egomaniac. A bit arrogant. I'd say that success had gone to his head."

"I take it you really didn't like him," I said.

"That's probably a bit strong. We tolerated each other."

"Did you ever help him with his act?"

He laughed. "I mean, look at me. Do I look like the sort of character who would look good on any stage?" he said.

I must admit, he did have a point. But what can you say? It's a bit like the missus asking you if her dress looks ugly.

"I wouldn't say that," I said. "Don Rickles never looked good, and he had a great career."

I knew it was completely the wrong thing to say. I mean, he had probably never even heard of Don Rickles.

"Well, I had not thought of stage work and that's the way I wanted it," he replied. "I did a bit of community theatre when I was a teenager, but that was about it.

"How do you get on with Marie?" I said.

"I wouldn't say we were close. She's a bit of an extravert but I am pretty comfortable with that. I can deal with most people."

At that point, I was aware that somebody was coming in from outside. The door opened. It was Marie.

"Gentleman, I believe you have met my brother-in-law."

Just another of those stupid statements. What did she think we'd been doing? Sitting there staring at each other, wondering who the fuck we were looking at.

"We have, indeed," I said.

"Sorry, I was not here. I've just been for a manicure."

Holy shit. She was actually having a manicure, not that I would have noticed the difference.

"Very nice too," I said. Look, I'm a guy. We know how to lie to women.

"I was just about to go out," said Baldipp.

"We won't keep you, sir," I said.

He put down his Styrofoam cup. He left, turning to smile at Marie on his way out.

"What is it this time?" asked Marie. To be honest, I've had enough of these questions.

"We want you to be honest," I said. "You haven't seen Mr. Horgan by any chance, have you?"

"Not since the day he left."

"And not heard from him?"

"Not a word. I think I told you I didn't expect to see him again."

"When did Mr. Baldipp arrive here?"

"Perhaps, ask him.".

"I already have. If you could answer the question."

"He arrived in Calgary yesterday evening."

"Has Mr. Baldipp ever helped Boudin with any of his illusions?"

"Not often, but yes, he has," she said. Hmmm.

"In what fashion?"

"Several illusions. Not for some time, though."

Very surprising. Why did Baldipp deny this, I thought?

"As a matter of interest, do you know where your husband's cell phone is?" I said.

"What a strange question. I can't be sure, but Mr. Horgan was using it the last I saw it."

"Good," I said. "I'm sure we'll find him eventually." I didn't add the word 'dead.

"Anything else, Mr. Arbuckle?" she said. "I do have to go to the bank this afternoon."'

"The Insurance company pay up?" I said. I know I was being a bit crass.

"As a matter of fact, they did. Well, the first of several payments they will be making."

"I know I'm being a bit blunt, Marie, but if you were to die, where would the money go?"

"I have written a will. It would go to my next of kin, though to be fair, I'm a bit bereft of relatives. I suppose it might go to Luke; He doesn't know that. It's certainly not something I'd want to discuss. Not something I've ever considered."

"Marie, do you have any other enemies?'

"What a strange question. None that I can think of. Should I have enemies?"

"We all have enemies somewhere. Knowing who they are in the big issue," I replied..

"Why are you asking this question?"

"Let's say I'm just covering all the bases."

"Look, I do have to go. I simply don't want to miss my appointment at the bank. I only came back here to pick up the relevant documents."

"Certainly. If I have any more questions, I'll give you a call."

"I hope you don't, Mr. Arbuckle. This is getting tiresome. I'll see you out.".

As I left, I picked up the Styrofoam cup that Baldipp had left on the desk. She did not appear to notice.

I followed her out. As I walked away, she got into her car and sped away, spitting out the gravel behind her. I hope she realized that this was a 50 km zone. I walked to the bus and climbed in.

'You've had a bit of an easy day here," I said to Red and Jen.

They had very little to report. But that was the life of a private investigator. Still, they were doing an important job. And I had some interesting things to tell them.

"I was contacted by Louie about an hour ago with some important news."

"It's getting to the point where everything is important," said Red. "What gives?"

"Louie told me that the police had received a phone call a couple of days ago. It was threatening. Essentially, it said bad things were going to happen to Mariel. Apparently, it was quite a violent message."

"Any idea who might be behind this?" said Red.

"Well, it was a male and a male who called using Boudin's cell phone."

"When did this happen?"

"About two days ago," I replied.

"Any ideas?"

Plenty of ideas Red, but no evidence. I suppose the obvious candidate would be Horgan. But it all seems a bit obvious to me. As if somebody wants us to think it was him. I mean, he could obviously use Boudin's phone. The question is, did he?

"Any calls since?' said Jen.

"I don't think so, but then again, it took the cops 48 hours before they released this information."

"Any other males who we know of?"

"Not really. I mean, there's that Baldipp guy."

"Yeah, we saw him drive away," said Jen.

"Why would it be him?" I replied. "He didn't arrive here from Medicine Hat until last night. How would he get hold of Boudin's phone? And what could he possibly have against Marie?"

"Good point. One thing is for sure. It wasn't Marie," I said.

"What about tonight? You want us to go in?" said Red.

"Nothing's changed guys. If you go after midnight. I want you to pick up the pizza box and garotte, and anything else you find interesting."

"I'll make sure I wear gloves and put everything in a plastic bag," he said.

"Way to go. You had a good teacher."

"A good teacher. Who the hell was that?" he said.

"Eat my..... "

Jen put her hand over my mouth. We laughed. I wasn't actually going to complete that sentence.

"Anyway, guys, I think they'll be gone for the day shortly. Just take it easy and be back just before midnight. One thing I would ask is that we keep in touch by cell phone while you're in there. This time the weather is better, and it should be a lot easier."

I'm not sure where they went, but I went straight home. There had been nothing to disturb my hunch. It was like all theories. There to disprove. It was still viable.

When I got home, Rita was getting a bit anxious. We were scheduled to go to the Private Investigators Annual Meeting. It was to be held at the top of the Calgary Tower. Interesting landmark that is shaped a bit like the Olympic Torch.

We rarely did these fancy events and I must admit that I'd quite forgotten about it. Not that I mentioned that to Rita. She'd taken about an hour and a half to get ready. It was time well spent. I said I was a guy, and it would take me twenty minutes and that included a shower. I wasn't one for formal events, and I knew my tuxedo wouldn't fit. This was a charity event. All the guys were asked to climb as many steps as they could. They would be led by a guide dog. Multiply the number of landings by ten dollars and the money was to be given to the Southern Alberta Guide Dog Association. I should add that there were 802 steps in this building. The women would wait in the restaurant at the top of the tower. I volunteered to go last. I had a pretty good idea of what was to happen. And it did. I threw up on the third landing. I said it was the guide dog, but I doubt anyone believed me. I had to go back down and take the elevator.

By the time I got to the restaurant, some of the speeches had started. Speeches bored the shit out of me, and the sound system didn't help. It was crap, but I was able to sit by the window and squeeze Rita's knee. The restaurant section revolved around 360 degrees, and it was great to see the lights of Calgary move slowly by. I could almost see the warehouse in the distance. I could definitely see the Bonnybrook Waste Disposal Plant. Fortunately, I was shielded from the smell.

We were sitting at a table along with a few guys and their wives. They were part of the Southeast Section. They had come from Lethbridge, Medicine Hat, and Pincher Creek. There was even a representative from the Piikani Indian Reserve. Good to see that, and I was disappointed that Red had not come.

It just so happened that I was sitting next to Ross Holder. I had known Ross for many years. He just so happened to be based in Medicine Hat. I don't enjoy mixing work with pleasure, but this was an opportunity. I took Ross to the bar and asked him if he knew Baldipp. He didn't have to think too hard. What he had to say was quite disturbing. He confirmed what my IT guy had told me about Baldipp, but said there had been some issues with this guy regarding child pornography and potential violence. It seems as if he had been put on probation at one time. I asked him if he could check up on this guy. Anything at all. When was this guy last seen? What sort of car did he drive, financial status? That sort of thing. He said he'd get right to it and report back to me. Oh, and he knew my IT guy and remembered his name. It was Rick McTavish. At least, I wouldn't have to call him Buddy anymore.

I told him Ross and I would pay him a fee. He refused. Private eyes are a bit of a club. We'd always help each other out.

One of my problems on this sort of occasion and, for that matter, Rita's, was that we tended to enjoy ourselves too much. That was why we'd always take a taxi. There were too many check stops these days. No use picking up a ticket. We'd enjoyed the evening and, in fact, were the last to leave. We stood looking down at the city and before I knew it; I was getting quite sentimental. Was it the booze or was there something else? I talked about our relationship and how much it meant. I suggested perhaps we change our status. My god, what was I doing? "You mean you're asking me to marry me," she said. "No," I said, "I'm wondering if I can go rent-free for the next few years." Ah, fuck it. She was right. That's exactly what I meant.

"What about a ring?" she said.

"You women expect everything all at once, but don't worry, I've got Amazon Prime. It will be here tomorrow."

She laughed. She thought I was joking.

I knew I would wake the following morning with a hangover. Hopefully not too bad. I didn't want a headache, and I didn't think I would. We took a taxi home. I was sort of in la-la land. And then the phone went.

Fuck, I'd forgotten all about Red and Jen. I would have to try and sound sober.

"What's happening, guys?" I said.

"It's Red here. I'm in the warehouse. I did as you said. Found some interesting shit in here. Might mean nothing, but I found some interesting props. A straight jacket, some cuffs, and something in the furnace. Don't know what it is."

"Where are you now?"

"I'm sitting on the wicker trunk going through some papers. Anyway, I'll get these up to Jen in just a moment. Will you be up when I get home? "

"I'll try to be," I said.

Shit, I was going to have to get the coffee percolator going. Then, a couple of minutes later, I called Red back. I wanted copies of Marie's bank statements if he could find them. But there was no answer. Not a problem. I'd see him in a couple of minutes. Except, I didn't. I collapsed into a coma and was gone for the night. They decided not to wake me.

19

LUKE BALDIPP

When I woke the following morning with a pounding headache, Rita was ready to greet me.

"You really meant what you said last night," she said.

"I wasn't being honest," I replied. "I don't have Amazon Prime. She had the frying pan in her hand and was ready to use it. A bad move for me." Of course, I meant it, I continued. "I'll only ask you once," I said. "I'm quite practiced at this marriage sort of thing. But what do they say? Practice makes perfect."

"She let the matter drop as she made coffee, but I didn't think it would lay fallow for long."

Red and Jen were understandably quite tired, and it was ten before they appeared. Of course, the big topic of conversation was my proposal the night before. Both Red and Jen seemed quite amused about it. I didn't think this was funny at all. Thank god, Rita didn't do Facebook or all the other social networks. That really would have pissed me off.

"So, tell us about the wedding," said Red.

I mean, I didn't want to talk about it. I wanted to ease into my new reality slowly. Rita understood and did her best to add a bit of levity.

"There's one thing I'll tell you, young man, I won't have to get married in white,"

"Perhaps Rita could borrow Jen's wedding dress," I said. Rita was ready for this.

"Honey," she said. "Elasticated fabric is so bloody expensive these days."

"But hair isn't," said Red. "He should get a hair transplant or a wig. You can get them cheap these days. It would take 5 years off him." They were taking the royal piss now.

"Bugger off Red," I said. "I need something that would take 15 years off me. I tried a wig once, but it was just too obvious.

We all laughed, though laughing was a bit more painful for me. I needed a handful of aspirins. That's it, I thought. I'll never get pissed again. How many times have I said that? Time to own up to the AA guy. But there was something in Red's comment that set me thinking.

After breakfast, it was time to analyze what Red had brought back. Fortunately, he had the wisdom to wear gloves and put everything in plastic bags. It was what he didn't bring back that seemed to be the most important.

"The warehouse safe had been left open," said Red. "There were packages in there containing a lot of money. And I mean a lot of money," he said.

"Marie must have cashed out her life insurance winnings," I replied. "The issue is why so quickly."

"I got the garotte and the pizza box and I also found a strait jacket and cuffs near the furnace. Might not be relevant at all."

"Let's get this to Louie, and I'll throw in the cup I picked up yesterday. Who knows what it might show? Maybe nothing. Maybe break the case."

"I don't know what this means, but there was something odd about the furnace."

"What do you mean?" I replied.

"They'd obviously been burning something in there. Don't know what it was, but I took a sample of white ash. I don't want to say anything more about that. It really could be anything."

"Very good," I said. "Oh, what's that white envelope you dropped on the table?"

"Sorry, I quite forgot about that. Let me empty the contents out for you."

Red carefully deposited several pieces of paper on the table.

"Looks like a cheque."

"Indeed, it is," he said

He carefully rearranged the pieces until they resembled a cheque. One or two pieces were missing, but it was certainly readable.

"Let me see. A cheque was written to Luke Baldipp for a thousand dollars."

"What was the date?" Red said.

"It was dated exactly two weeks ago. That was just before the big show at the Jube."

Red poured more carefully over the cheque. He studied it intently.

"This was written out by Boudin. All the details are in the same handwriting that I've seen before."

"Interesting. Marie had said Boudin just signed the cheques. It was her who filled them out."

"What the fuck was he doing writing out a cheque to Baldipp and why was it torn up?" I said.

"That's the big question," said Red. "Baldipp claims that he didn't arrive here until the last couple of days, but the cheque is dated two weeks ago. And why would Boudin be paying Baldipp and for what?"

"There's something seriously amiss here. Somebody is lying. And I'm beginning to think it's Baldipp"

As we were discussing this, my cell phone rang. It was Ross Holder In Medicine Hat.

"Ross, it was great meeting you last night. You obviously drove home right after the show."

"Always a boring trip, and especially so in the dark. I took turns driving with the wife." He didn't say the wife wasn't his. The one I remember was not Chinese. Not my business, though.

"What have you got for me?" I said.

"It might not be anything much, but I found out a few bits and pieces about Baldipp."

"Fire away."

"Well, he's not been seen for quite some time and by that, I mean about ten days."

"Interesting. Did you find out what sort of car he drives?"

"I did. An old beat-up black GMC Tracker. I don't think they make them anymore."

"And not a Merc?"

He laughed. "Definitely, not a Merc."

"Anything else?" I said.

"Yes, he's apparently trying to sell his house. Went on sale this week. Not done through a realtor, though. A private sale."

"Do you have any contact numbers for this guy?"

"I do." I jotted the number down.

"Look, if you find out anything else, don't hesitate to call me. And don't forget to send me a bill."

"Don't worry about it. You'd do the same for me sometime." I told you we were a bit of a club.

After he rang off, I sat in thought for a few seconds.

"Penny for your thoughts," said Jen

"This situation is getting more convoluted by the minute," I said. "This thing is like a hall of mirrors."

"Do tell Uncle Red all about it."

"OK. I'll try to summarize the situation. This guy Baldipp turned up here in Calgary about 36 hours ago. Says he's Boudin's stepbrother. Just here to help. Never attended the cremation. By all reports, he's a bit of an isolate. Drives a piece of shit but turns up at the warehouse driving a Merc."

"Probably leased," said Red.

"Or could be Boudin's," said Jen.

"Let me summarize," I replied. "This guy hasn't been seen In Medicine Hat for some time. Then we find Boudin wrote a cheque to him two weeks ago and then rips it up. But according to Baldipp, the reason he came to Calgary was to support Marie. When was Boudin going to give him the cheque? But here's the rub. Marie admits Luke has been in town for a couple of weeks and may have helped Boudin with his illusions in the past. I mean, someone's telling fibs here. We have to find out who and why."

"Just a minute," said Jen. "There's a spot of blood on the edge of the cheque. At least, I think it's blood."

So there was. We'd have to get that analyzed. Perhaps it was just red ink. We would have to see.

"Anyway, what are the plans for today?" said Red.

"Given the threats against Marie, I think what we do is to continue surveillance. You should first go by her house in Pump Hill and check to see if the BMW is there. If not, go over to the warehouse and see if you can spot the car there. If she's not there, call me urgently. I'll meet Louie at the Wild Rose Brewery just off Crowchild. Jesus, alcohol is the last thing I need right now. On second thoughts we can meet at Tims on Macleod Trail."

They had only been gone for a few minutes when I got an urgent call from Louie. There had been another urgent threat against Marie. It had just been phoned in. The caller was anonymous.

"You have no idea where the phone call originated?" I said.

"Unfortunately, I do," he answered. "Are you sitting down, Sid? This is going to be a shock."

"I'm immune to shock," I said. 'Where did it come from?"

"It came from your assistant's phone. It was Red."

"What the fuck," I said. "I'm not immune to that sort of thing. That simply can't be true."

"I'm afraid it is." It all sounded like bullshit to me. Talked about dying in the fires of hell and Satan. Crap like that.

"I've known Red for years. He is an outstanding bloke. He'd never do anything like this."

"I'll give you a little while to work this out. For old times' sake. But if you don't sort it out soon, we may have to detain him."

"Thanks, Louie," I said. "I'll do my best." Talk about coming out of left field and that stuff.

Moments later, Rita came by.

"You look white, honey," she said. "What's the matter?"

"I just found out what a ring costs these days."

She knew I was bullshitting, but I wasn't going to tell her about this news. She really liked Red. Jesus we all did. I decided it might be a good idea to call him. Surely, this was all a mistake. I dialled his number three times, but there was no answer. That just wasn't like him.

20
WHERE'S MY PHONE?

I eventually had to leave home to meet Louie. I felt completely numb. I never said another word to Rita. It was at times like this, I used to pour a stiff drink. Not anymore, and certainly not after last night. I turned the radio on, and some guy said, "We're all in this together." Fuck, I thought. Never a truer word.

I hoped that Louie would have better news. Like it had all been a stupid mistake. I had the stuff that Red had collected the previous night. It was sitting on the back seat. I would pass it on to Louie. For the time being, I didn't give a shit about anything.

Tim Hortons might be known as the working man's coffee house. It had started with a few shops in Ontario, but 50 years later, it had become a conglomerate and had even spread overseas. It was started by a hockey player. A bit before my time in Canada, but I got the impression that this guy was a bit more famous in death than he was in life. There weren't too many towns and villages in Canada that didn't have Tim'. I think that Macleod Trail had several. I hoped I was going to the right one. I often fucked up going to the right place. But not this time. As I arrived, Louie was just entering. I tooted my horn and beckoned him over. I obviously wasn't going to pass the stuff on in the coffee house. He got in my car.

"Any luck with Red?" he said.

"Not yet. He's not answering."

"I think we better contact Baldipp. If there is any danger to Marie, I think he should know."

"He's a bit of a conniving bastard that Baldipp," I said. But I did see his point.

"Want me to do it?"

"I'll do it," I said. "He knows who I am."

I carefully dialed Baldipp's number and there was an immediate response, but not what I expected.

"What's happening, boss?" said Red. "We've just arrived at the warehouse. No Marie, but Baldipp seems to be here."

"What the fuck are you doing answering that phone? It's not yours."

"Sure it.......... Oh, fuck. You're right, it looks just like mine."

"So, where the fuck is yours?" I said.

"I have no idea," he replied.

"Well, whoever has it just made a phone call threatening violence against Marie. When did you last have it?"

"Not this morning. I had it in the warehouse last night. Shit, I left it on the desk, I think, though I am sure I had picked it up."

"You picked a cell phone up all right, but it wasn't yours."

"Whose was it?"

"Luke Baldipp's."

"You're shitting me?"

"I shit you not," I said. "You're holding Luke Baldipp's phone.".

"Are you saying that Baldipp made a threat of violence against Marie?"

"Not necessarily. Somebody who had your phone contacted the police and made those threats."

"Well, who else could it have been?"

"I really can't think of anybody, to be honest," I said. "Look, I'll be over there quite soon, and we can talk more."

"I think I got the gist of that," said Louie. "You mean that the call came from someone else? Probably Baldipp."

"That's what Red said. I never had any doubts about the lad, but there's always that nagging suspicion. We should visit Mr. Baldipp and see if he has Red's phone."

"Who could have imagined that might happen? Odd that Red didn't notice," said Louie.

"If it was Baldipp who made the call, it was odd that he didn't notice."

"Hopefully, he doesn't notice any time soon. Anyway, it would be very interesting to look back through his history to see who he was calling and when."

"That's what I thought," I said. "I'll ask Red to write down the numbers of the last 30 calls made on that phone. And then we might think about getting the phone back to its rightful owner."

"Good idea, boss."

"Anyway, I do have a few things to pass on," I said to Louie. "I couldn't give them to you in there. Evidence and all that sort of thing. Let's see what fingerprints are on these things. See if we can find any blood or tissue or anything."

"I'll get it done urgently," he said. "I do have the senior detectives interested in this case. They are thinking of re-opening it. They have promised me full cooperation."

"Good to hear," I said. "Any luck with the sample I gave you yesterday?"

"Should have the results in a couple of hours. I'll call you when I have it."

"Please, if you could. I think it could break the case wide open."

We never did have coffee together. We had more important things to do. I went through the drive-through. A large extra dark roast would do the trick.

When I got to the warehouse, I first discussed strategy with Red and Jen. I explained the situation. Because of the threats, we had to get into the warehouse and talk to Baldipp. I'm sure he wouldn't admit to anything, but we had to ask. There were so many oddities about

Baldipp, and we had to sort them out. I asked for the list of calls that Baldipp or whoever had made on this phone.

We decided to use Marie's whereabouts as an excuse for the visit. There was no point in accusing Baldipp of making the threatening call. That might come later. But there was one thing bothering me. What exactly was he doing in the warehouse?

When we entered the warehouse, Baldipp was quite affable. Almost confident. It was when we showed him his cell phone, his mood changed.

"Sorry about this Mr. Baldipp, but when I was here yesterday, I picked up your phone by accident. Here it is." He looked puzzled and then shocked.

"I didn't realize it was missing. Well, I'm glad to get it back."

"I don't suppose you know where my phone went," said Red. "I thought I'd left it in here."

"Haven't got a clue," he said.

"So, you didn't use it?"

"'I think I would have realized right away," he said. I'm very careful with these sorts of things.

He looked shaken.

"Perhaps you could let me know if you find it," I said.

"Of course, I know how attached to our cell phones we all are," I added.

"There is one thing," I said. "When was the last time you saw Marie? There was another threatening message overnight."

I didn't want him to know that we had figured that it was almost certainly him. Just act dumb in these situations, which for me was not difficult.

We concluded the meeting quickly after that. Baldipp had been brazen throughout, even confident. The case had become even more confusing. There was going to be a key to all this that would unlock the puzzle.

When I got back to the bus, we went over what had happened. Before we did that, Jen had some interesting news for us. She had discovered that the black Merc was not Baldipp's but Boudin's. No idea how she had discovered this, but it seemed to make sense. Perhaps Marie had permitted him to use the car. That raised the question. Where was the Tracker? It certainly wasn't in Pump Hill. Unless he had caught the bus from Medicine Hat, it should be here. I did have an idea about this and sent Jen off to investigate. There were simply more questions than answers. We decided that this would be a waiting game, but we couldn't wait too long.

I decided it might be useful to call Marie on her cell phone. But despite three tries, there was nothing. I didn't leave a message. She was not the sort of person to ignore her phone. I'd always been able to get her before. It was only when I suggested we continue to surveil and possibly have another look around the warehouse that Red gave me a big surprise. Red had always been a Jack of All Trades. I mean, he could do anything. Repair my computer, rewire my house, tune my engine. He would even change the oil in my car, albeit once every two years. And he could reset the security system in the warehouse so that the back entrance was open even though it indicated locked. This meant I could get in and have a look around. No climbing down ropes which, let's face it could have been fatal for me. Absolutely brilliant.

Sometimes you have to get your priorities right. My immediate priority was to think about Rita's ring. I'd have a window of opportunity before supper. I mean, I'm a guy. I know fuck all about diamonds. One thing I know is that they're not as rare as people think but you still have to pay a fortune for a good one. I didn't have a fortune, but I had enough to get something decent.

I went down to this place on Macleod Trail. It wasn't quite Manny's House of Diamonds, and it wasn't De Beers. I walked in and was just about to ask if they had any good deals when my cell phone went off. I almost didn't answer it. It was my IT guy. Remember him. Rick McTavish. He was in for a conference and staying at the Carriage

House Hotel just up the road. I asked him if he was free for a few minutes. He was having a cocktail. He sounded as if he'd had several. Let's be honest, no one attends all the papers at a conference. I don't. I then called Red to find out if Baldipp was still there. He was. I picked up Rick at the Carriage House. He'd put a bit on a bit of weight since I last saw him. I'd put on a lot, and he did comment on that. I wasn't about to tell him what I was up to, but he went along with me.

It was only about a five-minute drive down to the warehouse. I just hoped Baldipp was still there. He was. The question is, would he come out anytime soon? He didn't. I told Rick there was somebody I'd like him to see and if our friend wouldn't come out, I wondered if he could go to the door. I mentioned in the end that I was looking for an identification of Baldipp. Would Baldipp recognize him? He thought not.

After waiting for about forty-five minutes, Rick walked up to the door. I told him to say he was looking for a charitable pledge for COVID-19 victims in Mongolia. I mean, I'd had quite a few of these requests in the last few months. Rick rang the buzzer outside the warehouse and waited. I couldn't see what was going on. I had parked about fifty yards away. I started to worry. What if Baldipp agreed to give some money? That could have been a problem. Baldipp essentially told him to come back when the woman of the house was there. That could be the next day or never. When Rick came back to the car, I needed to know if this was Baldipp.

"Rick," I said. "Could you positively identify this man as Baldipp?"

"I'm quite sure this was not Baldipp. I mean, there is a sort of resemblance."

"You mean the chrome dome," I said.

"Exactly. But he's just too relaxed and self-assured for Baldipp. So, who the fuck is this guy?" he demanded.

"That's the big question," I replied. "But I can tell you one thing. He's up to no good."

I dropped Rick off at the hotel. I took him for a drink. He had scotch. He didn't need one. I did, but I had a hot chocolate instead.

21

UNHEALTHY PIZZA

I went back to the warehouse. Baldipp or whoever the fuck he was, had gone. We'd go in there and have a look-see after we'd had some supper. But first, I had to get the bloody ring. I still had thirty minutes before the shop closed. And don't think I hadn't checked out Amazon. I had.

When I got there, the shop was full of anxiety ridden young men pretending to know what they were doing. One was with his mother. At least, I thought it was his mother. Some young guys feel safer with a more mature woman these days.

"How could I help you?" said a smarmy looking shop assistant. At least, he looked smarmy. I could imagine that superior look behind his designer mask.

"I'm looking for an engagement ring," I said

"Well, you've come to the right place, sir. We rather specialize in those things. Perhaps your son could give us some ideas."

Was he being a dick, or was this just the spiel they spouted every day?

"How much were you thinking of paying, sir?"

"How much?"

"Well, we do everything from the economic........" Of course, he meant cheap. ...." to the higher end. For those who think a ring is important."

He must have done this a thousand times. He'd make people pay a lot more than they could afford.

"I can see you care for your beloved."

"What could he see that I couldn't? Everybody was staring at me. Or so I thought."

I was beginning to feel nauseous. I really was. Was it the booze from the night before or the bullshit I was enduring? I have a ruse for this sort of situation when I'm uncomfortable. I have this device on my phone. You press this button and the phone rings.

"Hello," I said. "Go long on Apple. But don't bid it up."

Everybody was looking now. Who was this guy in boots, jeans, a leather jacket, and no socks?

"Oh, and if you could get that jerk, Elon Musk to give me a call."

I was tempted to say, "Get me half a dozen apples" but I would have pissed myself laughing.

I excused myself and left the store. It was going to be Amazon, after all. Take a look at their site. You can get some decent stuff there. I'm not shitting you and they take my credit card and deliver the goods the next day.

After I left the store, I went down to the Taj Mahal to meet Red and Jen. My favorite Indian Restaurant. We would have gone down to the Little Chief Restaurant in the Grey Eagle Resort Hotel. That was Red's favorite place. He used to work there, but it was just too far to go that night. We'd get there the following week. It was relaxed dining. Red and Jen were not too interested in really spicy things. I was all in on the Vindaloo Prawn Curry. It went from mild to only for the expert. Perhaps it was my English blood, but the expert version wasn't going to beat me. It nearly did. Perhaps it really was the booze from the night before.

In reality, the curry was not a good idea. The warehouse might have to wait a couple of hours. I didn't want to leave the pungent odor of curry in there. It would be a dead giveaway. We lingered over our meal. I paid for it with my credit card, but it wouldn't go through. Fuck. That was the card I was going to use for the ring. And then I realized it was an old card. Saved again.

We sat there for a few minutes looking at the numbers Baldipp had recently called. There were several calls to the police and one to customs and immigration. There was one call to Marie and there was a call to Baldipp's home number in Medicine Hat. I suppose he could have been checking an answering machine. He certainly wasn't calling himself. And that was about it.

When we got down to the warehouse, the area was deserted. Well, not quite. A couple of street people had broken into the bus. But we didn't care. It was a chilly night. They'd need a bit of shelter. We told them to stay there, but they had better fuck off in the morning.

It was easy to open the back entrance door. It was unlocked, as Red had suggested. No alarms went off. We just walked in. The furnace had not been tended to. It was out. There was nothing of interest in the back of the warehouse, but we spent quite a bit of time in the office. The pickings were slim but not insignificant. Red had been in here twice before. He sat on the wicker trunk watching proceedings and checking the social media. I went through the desk very carefully. There was not much to see. But there was something. There was a packet of very personal information. I opened a manila envelope and there was Baldipp's passport. The picture was certainly Baldipp. And there was an e-mail confirmation of a ticket to Canberra. He was to leave in forty-eight hours. That was not all. There was a considerable amount of cash and a bank draft for a hundred thousand dollars written to him. The thing that intrigued me was Marie's driving license, which was also in there. Why would he have it? A driving license is something I never let out of my sight, and I doubt she would. And there was a piece of gold jewelry. I can't say it was Marie's, but it was certainly pricey. Not the sort of thing I could get on Amazon. Rita would have been overjoyed with it. It was certainly difficult to come up with any different conclusion. I thought it was obvious.

After I checked everything in the office, we decided that was it for the night. When we got back, Rita was waiting for us. She asked me about the ring. I said she'd have a surprise the next day. If Amazon

Prime didn't come through, I'd be having a nasty surprise. And then I did have a surprise there and then. Louie had left a message on my cell phone. He told me to look at my e-mail. He had sent me some very interesting information. We got my laptop out and waited for it to load.

As we waited, Jen suddenly touched Red's pant leg. This was not an amorous gesture. She took her hand away and looked at it.

"Red," she said. "There are spots of blood on your trouser leg. Where the hell did that come from?"

"You sure it's blood?" he said.

She nodded. "Certainly, looks like it."

"I can't imagine. Perhaps I nicked myself in the warehouse."

"Perhaps there is another reason and if there is, we'd better find out quickly," I said.

As she said that, my computer beeped. I was ready to access my e-mail. There was a note there from Louie. It talked about the latest report from forensics. It was quite lengthy, but in essence, it made the following points. There had been fingerprint matching between the coffee cup that Baldipp had used and the pizza box we had found in the warehouse. There was also evidence of some tissue on the garotte and a small amount of blood. They could not at this point identify the source of that. Also, there were green woolen fibres found on the garotte and, somewhat surprisingly, on the straightjacket that we had found. Louie had described it as an unusual shade of green.

The most significant piece of information came last. Analysis of some of the ash found in the furnace suggested human bones. They might be able to identify that later. There was other stuff in there that was not significant. I'm not sure that we needed to know that there was evidence of a Hawaiian pizza in the pizza box and that there was no maker's name on the box. At the end of the report, Louie added that other results, such as blood analysis, would be available first thing in the morning.

This was all stunning news. We sat by the computer to work out what this all meant. It was Jen who was the first to speak.

"This might be circumstantial, but I think we can put two and two together," she said.

"I agree, I replied. "It looks like the pizza delivery guy who wasn't almost certainly wasn't a pizza guy at all and may have been involved in the killing of……

"Horgan," interjected Red. "I'm willing to bet that those green fibres came from Horgan's sweater. I mean, who the fuck wears that sort of green these days?"

"Exactly," I said. "Let's put it all together. Red tell me. What do you think the sequence of events was here?"

I think I'd already worked that out, but I wanted him to confirm my reasoning.

"Well, pizza man turns up at the warehouse. He obviously was there to murder Horgan. The issue is why?" said Red.

"Perhaps the pizza was late, and Horgan requested a two-for-one deal," I replied.

It was just too late for that sort of humour. They just ignored me.

"The pizza man walks in and when Horgan is not paying attention, he is attacked by the pizza man." continued Red.

"Would it be that easy," said Jen. "Perhaps that's where the straight jacket comes in. Marie gives him the chance to show his prowess. Remember, it seems as if he has pretensions to be an illusionist. If you're any good at this sort of thing, let's see if you can get out of the straight jacket."

"Heh, babe, you've got an amazing imagination, but who knows? You might be right. Proving it will be a bit of a bugger," said Red.

"All of this seems to suggest that Marie was in on this from the start. I mean, it's hardly likely that Horgan would somehow contact a pizza joint to send out a pizza man who just so happens to be a psychopathic killer," I said.

Red started laughing.

"I dunno. Some of those pizza guys can be a bit out there"

"Yeah," said Jen. "Like you Red. Didn't you do that at one time?"

Red laughed some more.

"I think we can guess the rest. Where to dispose of the body? The most obvious solution. The furnace. What pizza man doesn't understand is that even in a furnace, it is difficult to get rid of a body, at least completely."

"That's right," said Red. "When people get cremated, the body is incinerated for at least two hours at extreme temperatures and even then most of the long bones survive."

"I'm not sure we need to know that," said Jen, contorting her face.

Where the fuck does he get this sort of information? I thought to myself. It certainly wasn't in the writings of Voltaire.

"You know we keep talking about pizza man, but let's be realistic. The pizza man has to be Baldipp. It just has to be."

"Can we prove that?" said Jen.

"I think we can," I replied. "The fingerprints on the pizza box and the cup were the same. Unless we think he might have been drinking out of a dirty cup that somebody else had used, it's the only explanation. Red, do you agree?"

"Absolutely. So, what we have here is a plan by Marie and Boudin's stepbrother to eliminate Horgan. Now she was apparently having an affair with Horgan, so why would they conspire to kill him? "

"Perhaps he was bad in the sack," said Jen. I've met a few......I won't finish that statement.

She was joking, but I wasn't completely sure. By the look on Red's face, he wasn't sure either. A little jealousy does no harm.

"Marie was in it for the money," said Red. "She gets Horgan to bump off her husband. And the reward. The life insurance which she took out on his life. Boudin is dead. Horgan now becomes expendable."

"But why involve Baldipp, who she claims she hardly knows?" said Jen

"Good point," I replied. "She says that they had rarely met. He lived in Medicine Hat and wasn't exactly a good catch. He'd have to be pretty bent to get involved in this sort of thing. And what would be in it for him?"

"I suppose she could have paid him to do it, but it makes little sense, does it? A sort of murder for hire. I'm just not buying that," said Red.

"Didn't he assume that he might inherit if she died? There's always that," said Jen.

"Still doesn't make a lot of sense. Heh, Luke, come on over from Medicine Hat, kill my lover. Oh, and if I die, you'll inherit," I replied.

"That brings up another issue," said Red. "Where the fuck is Marie? We haven't seen her in a while and there are all these violent threats against her."

"Could be bullshit to lead us in the wrong direction," I said.

"Bullshit or not. Those violent threats likely came from Baldipp himself," Jen noted.

"The bottom line is whether the cops have enough information to arrest Baldipp for Horgan's murder," Red said. "What do you think, Sid?"

"I think they might. I'll talk to Louie about that in the morning," I said. "But the key thing here is to find Marie. I don't want to be morbid, but I do mean dead or alive.

"I think you're right," Red said. "And this is becoming a dangerous game. We're going to have to be prepared."

"You're suggesting we go to the warehouse in the morning," Jen said

"I think we have to," I replied. "We have to find Marie. I'm concerned. That blood on Red came from somewhere. We better find out where and quickly."

And that was it for the night. Rita pretty much insisted on that. It was two in the morning. I was just going into the bedroom when I heard Jen running back up the stairs.

"Sid, she said. How could I have forgotten?"

"Forgotten what?".

"I found the Tracker. It was left down the street at the Auto Dump a couple of weeks ago."

"Yes, how could you have forgotten?" I said. "Bedtime young lady."

Rita pulled me into the bedroom to put an end to any further discussion. It was not exactly a peaceful night. I tossed and turned, wondering about the implications of what we had just heard. I'm sure that was true for all of us. Perhaps we were all wrong, but the evidence for me seemed to be stacking up in only one direction. And that direction seemed inconceivable, but I couldn't rule it out.

22

HAMPERED

I was a bit bleary-eyed when I got up. I didn't sleep well. Over our first coffee, Rita told me she was going to pop out to Walmart to get some fancier face masks because of the pandemic. What's it with women? It's all about style. Got me thinking. Why do they put lipstick on to go out if they are wearing a mask? Regards masks, for me, it's just a question of durability. I've had my present one for three months. Why do I need another one? So long as you wash them every couple of weeks, what could go wrong? Anyway, Rita gulped down her coffee and left for Walmart. She was back in less than a minute. Only made it to the front door.

"What's this package from Amazon? I had to sign for it?".

Oh shit, I thought. She's just signed for her own engagement ring.

"Top of the line ink for my printer," I said.

"But you only print in black," she said.

"That's because I haven't got any coloured ink, my love."

I knew this conversation couldn't last; I tried the true and tested strategy of changing the subject.

"While you're down at Walmart, could you get me a packet of cigs?"

I knew that was a red rag to a bull, and it worked.

"Bugger off," she said as she slammed the door.

I carefully opened the box to reveal what I considered to be a beautiful ring. It was the right price. It was on special for the month.

Now, regarding price, there is a formula for working this out. Two times your monthly salary. Didn't work for me. On a bad month, I earned fuck all. No, it looked quite flashy to me. It was a diamond, but I have to be honest, the Zirconia looked just as good.

I must admit the cost bothered me somewhat. Rita had been having trouble with her teeth and urgently needed some dental implants. The cost was about the same. But could you imagine saying 'With these dental implants, I do thee wed' Don't tell Rita I said this.

I didn't wait for Rita to come back to have a bite to eat. It wasn't that I was on a health kick, but it was on doctor's orders. I'd start the day with All-Bran. Tasted like granulated cardboard but it kept me regular. Apparently, that was good if you were watching the clock all the time.

I was halfway through breakfast when Red and Jen emerged. I knew it was very likely that Louie would have called, and I was tempted to finish the second half of my bran in record time. That would have been anything under half an hour for that stuff. I had just poured a coffee for Red and Jen when Rita emerged with her new mask. It was very colorful. I'd never lose her in the dark again. There's an idea. Luminous face masks. Anyway, what was more important? Louie's news or the ring. I'm not completely stupid. I sent the guys back downstairs to talk about the case.

I must admit when I was in the jeweler's the day, I was not completely dumb. I whipped a shopping bag from the counter and filled it with their advertising blurb. I mean, they weren't going to stop me on the way out and accuse me of stealing their adverts. So, I carefully inserted the little ring box in the jeweler's bag and waited for her to appear. She did and fortunately, she had kept her teeth in. Nah, I'm just joshing with you. She looked radiant-ish. I'd like to say that this was the first time I had got down on my knee to propose. But I knew this would have to be the last time. Arthritis was setting in and getting up would be a problem.

"Sweetheart," I said. "Will you marry me?"

I tried to sound sincere, and I suppose I was.

"Yes," she said.

I mean, I would have been fucked if she'd said no. Amazon had said definitely no returns.

We did the big hug thing and I think I saw a tear in her eye. I knew how she felt. I felt a tear in my eye. My knee was really playing up.

And that was it. Well, almost. She asked me if I had a receipt for the ring. I hoped she wasn't thinking of flogging it. I told her I was so sure she would say yes, that I'd thrown it away. Nice move. Then, I asked her when she was going to do a cooked breakfast. I was hungry. Bad move.

The moment was saved when Red and Jen appeared. Rita was only too anxious to tell them about the ring, and Jen was eager to see it. I'm glad I did what I did. She'd probably know the difference between Zirconia and a diamond.

Rita eventually went into the kitchen to cook some breakfast. I know that sounds sort of bad, but we had to open up the computer and see what Louie had said. We had no time to lose.

I opened up the computer, and the message was there. It was quite long so I will get to the important points only. There was a lot of scientific gibberish in there to me. The blood analysis had been completed, and the results were partially in. It seemed as if the blood on the Pumphouse stage in front of the cabinet on the left side of the stage was not the same as the blood found in the vials which we were led to believe was Boudins. Of course, Marie could have been bullshitting us. But the blood on the cheque pieces written to Baldipp, which we thought might be red ink, was the same as the blood found on the stage floor. The blood found on the last will and testament was also the same as the blood on the floor but was identical to the blood in the vials. Finally, the blood on the knife was the same as the blood on the floor and almost certainly was the murder weapon. We'd have to think about what this all meant. Part of this just made little sense to my simple mind. And it had to, and quickly.

I've simplified this, but what the fuck did it all mean? I had something sitting at the back of my mind, but I wasn't going to say anything. I immediately contacted Louie and asked if he could send a photograph of the last will and testament card that had not been doused with blood. He said that he didn't have it and then I remembered it was in the trunk of my car. Before I rang off, I told Louie to get his arse down to the Auto Dump place and see if he could lift some prints from the car.

I left Red and Jen upstairs and went down to my car. It was unlocked. Hell, it was always unlocked. The locks fucked up about five years ago. I retrieved the card and went back upstairs.

"Honey," I said, "Any idea where I put the copies of the cheques that we got from Marie?"

"You put them in your briefcase. It's at the end of the bed."

It might have taken me half an hour to find them. This, of course, is what good women are made of. Looking after the inefficiencies of men.

"You've read the latest report. What do you guys think?" I said.

"Hmm, just trying to get my head around this," said Red.

"Me too. Just give me a moment," said Jen. "I'm just trying to process this."

As they were saying this, I was comparing the signatures on the cheques and the signature on the last will and testament card, the one that wasn't stained with blood. Holy fuck. They were the same. This was important. I told the guys to consider this first.

"What does it mean?" I said.

"I know this may sound stupid," said Jen. "I have this weird idea."

"Do tell," I said.

"If the signatures on this card and the cheques were the same and assuming that it was Boudin's signature on the cheques, it suggests that Boudin was actually in the cabinet on the right side of the stage."

"How did the other card get into the cabinet on the left side of the stage?"

"That's pretty easy," I said. "It was already there."

"Let me see if I'm getting this right. We know that unless Boudin dematerialized as per Houdini, he couldn't have got from the right cabinet to the left cabinet."

"That's right. Which means that............"

"It was someone other than Boudin who died."

"Very likely," I said. "And then there's the blood evidence."

"That's the most interesting part of this," said Red. "The blood work would also seem to support the fact that it was not Boudin who died. To do so, we have to assume that the blood in the vials was Boudin's, as Marie alleged."

"Who else would it be?" said Jen. "They weren't running a blood transfusion service."

"It also suggests that whoever died was carrying the cheque we found. It was written to Baldipp and tinged with blood. I just can't see any other explanation. Why was the blood on the last will and testament, the one that was tinged with blood, the same as that in the vials?" said Red. "Always assuming that was Boudin's blood in the vials."

"That's a problem with the whole thesis," replied Jen.

I thought I could answer that.

"I think what happened here was that the murdered man pitched forward onto his face. We both saw that, but the knife was in his back. Now it is possible that blood seeped through to the front, but I doubt it. I think they must have put Boudin's blood on the card later."

"Any other thoughts, guys?" said Red.

"I think I might be speculating a bit, but this is still the way I see it," said Jen. "Marie bumps off her husband."

"Stop there," said Red. "Marie arranges for Horgan to bump off who he thinks is her husband."

"That's right," I said. "I think we had already concluded that Bergman was Horgan. They were both in the cabinet on the left side of the stage and he does the stabbing. She uses her sexual wiles with

Horgan to achieve this. When he has fulfilled his usefulness, she arranges to have him bumped off. The black widow, so to speak."

"That's right," said Jen. "I think it's obvious. She uses someone else to bump him off. She's in the clear. Then comes the life insurance and life should be happy thereafter, especially with Horgan out of the way. And according to this thesis, Boudin must still be alive.

"So, who the fuck was murdered, Red?" I said.

"I'm not sure we know. Perhaps we will never know. He's been cremated."

"And where the hell is Boudin now?" I replied.‘

"Maybe long gone," said Red.

"Look. There are still two issues. Where is Marie and who the fuck is Baldipp?"

"I hope we soon find out," said Red. "Like you, Sid, I am very worried about Marie. I am really concerned about her, even though she is probably involved in two murders."

"I wonder if she had life insurance," said Red.

"Let's not complicate things too much," I said. "Let's worry about what we have to worry about. We have to get down to the warehouse."

"Who's paying for all of this?" said Jen.

"As a matter of fact, I am. Let's call it public service. But I'll be honest. If we solve this case, it could be very good for business."

"What time will we leave?" said Red.

"I think about now. That should do the trick. If he's there, that's fine. If he's not, we can wait until he arrives."

We were all ready to go when I received a call from Louie.

"Holy shit, Louie. That was quick. What have you got for me?"

"We've moved quickly on the case. The senior staff is all over it. I better tell you they are a bit pissed about being beaten to the punch by a low-level private eye."

I resented that comment. There was no need for it, though I knew Louie was only quoting his superiors.

"Any news?"

"Yes, there is. We had a look at the Tracker. Pieces were disappearing by the minute. It had been there about a week, but we got some prints."

"And the result, Louie?"

"They matched the prints on the pizza box. Make of that what you will."

"Over and out," I said. "I'll keep in touch."

The others were looking at me expectantly.

"That nails it," I said. "Horgan's killer was definitely Baldipp, or whoever he is. If Baldipp is a killer, we will have to be careful down at the warehouse. He won't hesitate to do it again."

"O.K captain," said Red. "Lead the way. By the way, where is Dave when you need him?"

Big Dave was Red's ex tag team partner. Solid physically as well as cognitively. The sort of 'Shall I hit him boss?' We'd interviewed him and were thinking about him. We should have been more decisive. "Out of town doing repossessions. We'll have to do it ourselves," I replied.

I let them go first because I wanted to say goodbye to Rita. I can be quite sentimental at times, though you might not have guessed it. I told her how much I loved her and was delighted she had accepted my offer. Jesus, did I say that? But look, I really meant it. This could be an iffy assignment, possibly my last. There was danger in the air.

We arrived at the warehouse after a slight detour to Tims. With the furnace out, it was likely to be cold in the warehouse. We needed something to keep us warm. Before we went in, I pointed out again that it could be a dangerous situation. I suggested it would be best for Red and me to go in and for Jen to go up top on the roof to keep an eye on what was happening below.

As we walked into the building, we were suddenly aware of the smell of gasoline. Not sure what this was all about. We walked into the office area. There was nobody there. We would sit and wait for Baldipp, or whoever he was. I'm not sure why I did this, but I thought

I would call the Boudin warehouse line. I had always contacted Marie through her cell phone. I dialed the number and heard the cell phone kick in.

"Hello, this is Pierre Boudin here. This is Boudin Enterprises. Please leave a message or s-s-s end me a message through the internet."

"So that's the silent illusionist," said Red

He might not have said much, but there was something significant in that message. I kept it to myself.

We sat there for a couple of hours. I sat at the desk. Red sat on the wicker trunk. We occasionally called Jen, who peered through the skylight. It must have been cold up there, but Jen was not the complaining type. There was one big concern. Had our friend already flown the coop? We hoped not.

I thought about sending out for a pizza but decided against it. Ordering pizza in that place could be a threatening enterprise. I tried reading a magazine called The Prestidigitation Periodical, but I was sliding into a drowsy state when suddenly Red let out a yell.

"Oh fuck," he said. "I know where that blood on my pants came from."

He stood there holding the open lid of the wicker trunk. I walked over to it. There was the body of Marie. She has been stuffed in the trunk. We should have noticed the pool of blood that had congealed under the trunk lid.. She looked as if she had been dead for some time. The signs of rigor mortis were definitely there, though I never touched the body. I'm squeamish about that sort of thing. I left that task to Red. We never found out how she had died, but it had obviously been a violent death. Red slowly lowered the lid. He didn't look too good, and I definitely didn't feel too good. I had seen death many times, but you never really got used to it.

Our suspicions about Marie's potential demise had come true. We now had to wait for the murderer to appear. We didn't have to wait long. Jen gave us a warning that he had just arrived in the Merc.

Moments later, he walked in. He was carrying a small case and a gas can. He didn't see us at first and then was startled when he did so.

"What the fuck are you doing in here?" he said. "How the hell did you get in?"

"Somebody didn't secure the back door," said Red, which I suppose was true.

"This is a private establishment," he said. "So, you will understand why I am asking you to leave."

When we have talked to you for a few minutes, you'll see why we won't.

I peered up towards Jen. She was keeping out of sight.

"I will give you a few minutes. I'm in a hurry. I have a plane to catch." That was true. He didn't mention it was the next day.

"I must admit, sir, you have led us quite a dance. The first issue is to find out exactly who you are."

"You know damn well that I'm Luke Baldipp."

"Well, you're acting the part of Luke Baldipp, but I'll come to the point. You are, in fact, Pierre Boudin, the silent illusionist, or should I say Doug Horton from Medicine Hat. Not very gallic, is it?"

"How can you possibly come out with these absurd ideas? You've been watching too much TV. This is p-p-preposterous." He tried to smile, but it was very forced.

"Pierre Boudin, the famous illusionist, was silent for many years. And why? He had a severe stutter as a child. You have certainly overcome your stutter, as most people do, but there are still remnants. And that Mr. Horton is not p-p-preposterous. "

"This is crazy. I am Boudin's stepbrother, so I am not completely related to him. I stuttered badly as a child. Others in our family did. This is no proof at all."

"On its own, I would agree with you, but there is much more to come," I said.

"These are just the rantings of a delusional fool. If you were at all serious, the police would be here. This wouldn't be left to a has-been private investigator and his sidekick."

At this point, Red stood up. Horton better not say something like that again. Red could tear him to pieces with one hand.

"Has been he might be. But I am very serious. The police are on their way," said Red.

I glanced up towards Jen as Horton stared at Red. He must have thought he had gone too far. And perhaps he was right.

"Look, if you don't mind, I have to leave," he said. "The police can interview me later.".

Red moved over to the door to bar his way.

"The police will be here in about twenty minutes and there will be no leaving," I said.

Of course, this was bullshit. I had no way of knowing that.

"Sit down, Mr.......what would you prefer Horton or Boudin?"

"Now look Indian. I don't know how you got involved, but you are out of your depth. You should have stayed on the reservation."

The Indian bit really pissed me off. Before my heart attack, I would have decked him. This guy was an arrogant prick, I thought. Insult my friend, you're insulting me.

I could see that Red was ready to explode. But he didn't. Good thing. That wouldn't have helped the situation at all. We didn't want another murder. Boudin sat down behind the desk.

"While we wait," I said. "I'll tell you exactly what I think happened here. Of course, you know this, but I want you to understand that we have worked this out, almost to the last detail."

This would take a few educated guesses, but I knew I wouldn't be completely wrong.

"It was a very clever plot," I said. "Convince the world that there is a madman loose who is threatening Boudin. Stage the murder at the Pumphouse Theatre. And who was murdered? Your stepbrother Luke

Baldipp. The next step, get rid of the guy in the audience. What was his name?"

"Peter Bergman," said Red. "And let's not forget Leonard Parr. At least he's still alive and talking."

"That's right. Get Marie to promise the guy big bucks to play the part of Horsfall, commit murder, and then get rid of him and dump his body in the Bow River. Not suicide. Almost certainly murder. Almost a crime of passion.Dead men tell no tales. Which is why Horgan had to go as well. I wondered about him. I suspect that the affair with Marie was all bullshit. She was probably leading him on. A quick call to you, a pizza box, and a garotte, and the poor bastard wouldn't be publishing any kiss-and-tell stories. Of course, what to do with the body? A bit too dangerous to carry him out. The next best alternative. Toss him into the furnace. Ashes to ashes and all that. Except we could identify those ashes. I must admit, the next bit confused me for a while. Why get rid of Marie? Perhaps, she was after a bigger cut of the pie. Perhaps she thought of blackmailing you. Perhaps we'll never know. But one thing's for sure. Marie is dead."

I went to the trunk and lifted the lid. Horton didn't flinch for a moment.

"But then you'd know all of this," I said. "Because you murdered her." Of course, at that point, I couldn't prove a darn thing. I didn't even know how or when she had died.

"You come here with your fancy fairy stories and expect me, and should I add the police, to believe these delusional ravings," said Boudin. "You have absolutely no proof. This story would be laughed out of court in ten minutes."

"Let's talk about the proof. It was not your blood on the stage floor. I mean that is rather damming. A dead man who doesn't have Boudin's blood. A bit tricky that. And your signature on the last will and testament card as you moved to the cabinet on the right side of the stage. It was your writing. While some people might believe you can cross the ether from one side of the stage to the other, we both know that's crap. Your rather sad stepbrother was in the cabinet on the left and it was him who died."

"Is that all?" he said. "It's all getting rather boring. This is a fantasy."

"No fantasy, Mr. Horton. None of this bullshit anymore. Let me tell you about the DNA evidence," I said.

Of course, this was complete bullshit. We didn't have it yet and there was no guarantee that it would show what we wanted. But he didn't know that.

"The evidence shows that the dead person at the theatre was not you. DNA analysis taken from the body indicates that it came from your stepbrother. Your DNA was nowhere to be found. I think you'll agree this is rather damning"

"And where did you get my DNA? I didn't give that to anyone."

"Yes, you did," said Red. "You left it on your coffee cup a couple of days back."

Suddenly, Horton's composure faltered. He began to fidget.

"You think you've got all the answers, don't you? Well, there is something you private eyes won't have an answer for."

He reached into one of the desk drawers and pulled out a pistol. It could have been a starter pistol for all I knew. I was taking no chances. He had killed before. He wouldn't hesitate to do it again.

"Both of you. Sit on the trunk where I can see you. Don't think of moving."

And then, before us, he began to change his appearance. He kicked off his shoes and began to change into Boudin. He took a wig out of his suitcase and deftly placed it on his head and then followed the mustache. Hell, this would look out of place in downtown Calgary, but it looked as if he had other disguises in his case. The transformation was remarkable. He had suddenly become someone else. He wore the dark black suit that he had worn on the stage. Not quite what you'd expect to see walking down Blackfoot Trail and not what the police would be expecting.

It was obvious he was going to do a runner. But what was he going to do to us? We soon found out.

"Gentleman," he said. "I have a choice to make. Your analysis of this situation was almost completely accurate, give or take one or two insignificant details. But the issue is what to do with you two. I could pump you full of bullets, but I think that would be rather obvious to anyone investigating. Don't want to be charged with your murder. I'm going to make this look like a complete accident."

I wondered what he meant until he produced the gasoline can from behind his desk. He went around the room, splashing gasoline all over the place, especially in a circle around us. Moments later He then stepped back, so he had access to the door. He then took out a lighter and set the room alight. He flipped the lighter to me. It said, "A gift from the Great Boudin". Bastard. At least, he didn't dowse us with gasoline. And then he was gone. The issue was how the fuck were we going to get out? The flames were licking at our feet when Jen smashed through the skylight above our heads and lowered a rope. Red was quick to clamber up and then they lowered the rope. There was no way I could climb it, but I hung on and they hauled me up.. By this time, I was feeling scorched, but at least I got out alive. I was getting this odd pain down my left arm. Perhaps it was indigestion again.

"Did you call the police?" I said to Jen.

"I did. They would have been here by now, but they got delayed by a goods train off Blackfoot Trail. You know how slowly they can clear a crossing."

"Shit!" I said. "He's going to get away."

And we had to get away quickly. The warehouse was fully ablaze. We clambered down to the ground and scuttled away to a decent distance from the warehouse. Goodness, what was in there? I didn't want to get caught in an explosion.

The police arrived a moment later. I could hear fire engines in the distance. It was Louie who dashed over to us. A couple of constables followed him.

"Jen called me and told me what was happening. We got here just as soon as we could. I guess he's gone."

"Any idea what he was driving?'.

"Probably a black Merc," I said. "I think Jen's got the plate number."

"'Don't worry," he said. "We'll pick him up pretty damn quick. Look, why don't we pop into the Blackfoot Diner? It's open 24 hours. You can tell me what happened over a coffee."

We took our respective cars and went down to the Diner. That place was good any time of the day and I knew I could cadge a cig from one of the girls there. We sat down and, while none of us felt like eating, Louie ordered a cheese omelet. Three coffees, no cream, was good enough for us. We carefully went through what had happened. Louie asked us if there was any way we could prove what had happened in the warehouse. Red placed his phone on the table. It's all there, he said. I recorded it.

"Just a minute," said Louie. "I thought you had lost your phone."

"I found it in the wastebasket in there," said Red. "At least, I think it's mine." We all laughed.

We were back home minutes later. Rita was waiting to see us. Jesus, I was glad to see her. It had been a tough night. I was stressed out. Red told me we should do a sweat lodge in the next day or so. I was up to it. Perhaps it would get rid of this fucking pain in my left arm.

23

THE TUNNEL

We slept in the following morning. I had to cancel a meeting for our next contract. That wouldn't go down well. They could easily go elsewhere. I fully expected that Boudin would have been caught by now. I called Louie to confirm this, but he couldn't. He said that a black Merc matching our description had been ditched on the outskirts of downtown. There was a check stop there that had nothing to do with the APB on Horton, but Horton had dumped the car and disappeared into the night. They had checked in on his house in Pump Hill. I mean, they had to, but inevitably he wasn't going to go back there.

The police were also visiting all the hotels downtown, but with no luck. They would be at the airport later that day. Remember, he had a ticket for Canberra, but he was hardly likely to consider that. I also knew they would check most of the highways. In my mind, this guy was probably trapped. It was just a matter of time.

Louie told me that the firemen had done a brilliant job and saved a good part of the building, including Marie's body. Red mentioned later that most illusionists spray many of their illusions with flameproof paint. Apparently, the history of illusions was littered with unnecessary and often fatal fires. This had saved the fire from spreading more than it did.

Although we considered we were now off the case, we couldn't let it go. As we had breakfast that morning, we speculated on just what

Boudin would do. Hell, it was difficult to call him by his real name. We kept forgetting.

We went over the case from the very beginning. It was now clear that Marie had set the whole thing up with her husband. The Eric Horsfall threats were complete bullshit. The notes were probably written by Boudin. The writing was certainly similar. They had rented the room in Inglewood, and the shadowy figure who had been seen on camera was probably Boudin. Only Marie could have told him about the camera. Marie had conspired with Horgan to kill who he assumed was Boudin. Some people would do anything for love or money, and he did. He had no idea that he had killed Baldipp. Horgan had to be erased from the equation, and he was by Boudin. Money is a great temptation, and so it was for Boudin. I imagine business had not been going well. Marie was expendable. Perhaps Boudin had somebody else on the side. We'd probably never know. The big remaining issue was where the fuck was Boudin now?

There was a consensus that he'd hardly consider going to a hotel. And an equal consensus that he would try to avoid public transport. There was another factor. What would he actually look like? He was hardly going to look like Boudin. That would stand out like a sore thumb. But what? My suggestion was that he would revert to looking like Baldipp. Looking like that, he could mingle anywhere.

I contacted Louie to mention this, and he was very grateful. They had no reports of anyone looking like a stage illusionist, but they might have better luck with some bald-headed coot who could have passed as a garden gnome wearing a mask. I know I was being nasty, but this guy was pissing me off. It was a personal vendetta now.

We all realized that the chances of us catching this guy were slim, but we knew what we were looking for. The rest of the day was spent catching up with paperwork and rescheduling some of our other contracts and leads. We got one from this executive who thought his wife was doing the cable guy. Didn't know they still had cable guys. Rita was visiting the neighbours, making sure they saw the ring. I couldn't wear a ring. I'd play around with them. I'd already lost two wedding rings, not that I needed them anymore.

And then we received a call from a TV news desk. Could we all do an interview on this fast-breaking story? They wanted us to appear on the early evening news. Sounded interesting, but part of being a private eye was being anonymous. If they'd filmed us at Walid's Falafel van, or the dilapidated school bus, our cover there would have been blown forever. We decided to do an interview, but we would let them use Jen. She was considerably better on the eye and more verbally sophisticated than we ever could be. We told her not to go into specifics. No need to mention us guys. I asked Red if he could record it.

The pain in my arm was not getting much better. I decided to pop into the Medical Clinic and check out the pain I had been experiencing.

My visit to the doctor was much like any other. Walk in, wait 15 minutes in a room to be told that I was probably suffering from esophageal reflux. He told me to keep social distancing and not to forget my mask. I mean, how the fuck can esophageal reflux be catching? I should also point out that he intimated I was a non-essential case. It was obvious he was telling me to piss off.

When I got home, the guys were all waiting for me. They were sitting around the TV. Red, bless him, had recorded the newscast. I must admit that Jen looked fantastic. Red said the make-up department had done a great job. I told him he'd better not mention that. Just say how fantastic she looked. The news was, as it always is these days, all about COVID-19 and the pandemic, and then, for a change of pace, news about how everybody needed to be vaccinated. They could fuck off as far I was concerned. Never needed them in the old days and we seemed to do alright. Besides, I reacted badly to pressure.

The piece on Boudin came at the end of the broadcast. It was done on the banks of the Bow River near the Drop-In Centre. Not sure that had to do with anything. Probably irrelevant. The piece started with a flashback to the tragic life of Pierre Boudin. They made him sound like the best thing since Houdini. Then Jen was asked to describe what had happened the night before. It only lasted about a minute and even then they cut her off. She never mentioned us at all, which was good. An advert followed it for fire extinguishers, which was ironic. We decided to watch it one more time. I mean, when it's a friend, you usually do. It was towards the end of the clip when Red noticed something.

"Just stop it there. Roll it back a few seconds."

Jen obliged.

"What are you looking for?" I asked.

"Look there. Immediately behind the interviewer. Just by the riverbank. You can see him next to the runner doing stretches."

"See him," said Jen.

"See who?"

"How many short, arsed bald guys wear a suit like that?" he said

"Jesus, you're absolutely right," she replied. "Can't see his face, but that simply has to be Boudin."

The guy was about to turn round when the TV cut away to the adverts.

"What do you think?" I said.

They both nodded. But what to do about it? We decided the guy might be staying in the Calgary Drop-In Centre, which was about fifty yards from where we saw him. You could see the Centre in the background. What a brilliant idea. Who would ever think of hiding in there? Boudin obviously had thought about it.

The Drop-in Centre was quite a modern facility that tended to cater on an emergency basis for the neediest in society. Guys would line up for several hours to get in there on wintry days. I mean, the accommodation was quite good, but it was getting quite crowded in there with the onset of winter. Boudin might take a bit of finding. We could only hope he was still there.

We decided to go down there right away. I suppose we could have called the cops, but we knew exactly who we were looking for. They only had a rough idea. We took Jen's car down there. It was easy to park and at least it would not quit in the middle of a journey. And parking was really easy. Since the Covid stuff had taken over, parking was free. They were almost begging you to go downtown. I should note we were not the only folks out that night. There was a big demonstration planned for the City Hall plaza. Something to do with civil rights and lockdowns. They seemed to happen every night. That was several blocks south of us, but we could see the crowds spilling into adjoining streets.

The Drop-In Centre was well organized. You just couldn't turn up and demand food and lodging. There was an information desk where people had to register. That was just what we needed; I went up to the desk. A young woman was sitting there.

"Excuse me," I said. "We're involved in a murder investigation and we're looking to see if a suspect is staying here."

"I'll have to see your identification. Besides, we're full," she said.

I admit I was looking scruffy, and the identification was a bit of a problem. I didn't even have my driving license with me.

And that might have been it, but moments later the door opened, and in walked somebody I knew very well.

"Bobby...for fuck's sake. What are you doing here? It's my old pal Bobby Horowitz," I said as I pointed at him.

"I'm sure he would have said Jesus Christ. It's you, Sid. But said person was not part of his vocabulary or his religion."

"Sid, so long, no see. What are you doing here?"

Now I better tell you about Horowitz. A few thousand bucks to Bobby would be a rounding-up error. He'd given a lot to charity over the years, much of it anonymously. He made his money the old-fashioned way. Fucking well worked for it, and hard.

"Look buddy, I need to check someone out in there. And we'll need your security guys."

I am not sure that Bobby had any push apart from his personality, but he got us in, along with a couple of beefy security guys. We went up to the first floor in search of our target. It was crowded, but there he was. Sitting on a bed reading a newspaper. His back was to us. He was wearing a dark suit and pants. He looked a bit out of place in there, but the centre was not a fashion show. I didn't think it would be this easy. We slowly approached and, without hesitation, grabbed him by the shoulders. He immediately turned to face us.

"What the fuck. Piss off, you arseholes," he said.

I mean, there was no doubt this was not Boudin. The complete absence of teeth should have been the first clue.

"Sorry mate," I said. "But where the hell did you get these clothes?"

"Don't matter man. They're mine now."

"Look, my friend, it does matter. This is a murder investigation."

I took out a fifty-dollar bill and waved it at him. I felt bad about that, but we had to know.

"Where do you get those clothes?"

"A guy who was in here last night paid me fifty bucks to swap clothes with him. Fuck knows why. But he was insistent."

"What clothes were you wearing?" I asked.

"Dark blue hoody, jeans, and runners with holes in them."

Shit, now he wouldn't exactly stand out in a crowd, would he? That was disappointing, but I was determined to find this guy. There was one thing though, the fella who donated the clothes was now a hundred bucks better off. And so was the Centre. I dropped a hundred-buck note in their donation box.

The issue was where would Boudin go now. Probably not to Pump Hill. I suspected he wouldn't go very far for now. He didn't have a car and I'm sure that public transportation was being watched. We essentially sat on our hands for the next 24 hours. The police were having no luck. And then we caught a break. Bobby Horowitz called me. He said that the guy from last night had told him he had seen Boudin sitting by the Calgary Olympic Plaza. He had approached him and asked for his clothes back. I mean, wandering around Calgary dressed like an illusionist was probably not ideal for a vagrant. Tough to tell people you were down on your luck. Boudin told him to bugger off or pay him back the $50 from the night before. He obviously didn't have that anymore. Our guy walked back to the drop-in centre and, fortunately, he bumped into Bobby by the front entrance.

I knew that we only had a few minutes to get there. We jumped in my car and hoped that the relative absence of oil would not cause us to stall on the way. We illegally parked on MacLeod Trail and ran towards the Plaza. Several vagrants were standing around in blue hoodies, but after about 10 minutes, we spotted Boudin. Unfortunately, he spotted us at the same time and set off running across the Plaza. We chased him but this was a bit of a problem for us all because the Plaza had a few icy patches and there also appeared to be some sort of demonstration in the offing. I'd like to say I was in hot pursuit. I didn't have a jacket, so it was more like cold pursuit. Red seemed to be gaining on Boudin, but he was still some way away when Boudin ran down the LRT tunnel heading south. This was a dangerous manoeuvre. You could easily get hit by a train and several had been over the years. The tunnel was about four hundred yards long.

When I saw him do this, I called Louie to get the police to the south end of the tunnel near Stampede Park. He said that they could be there within two minutes. This would not be enough time for Boudin to clear the tunnel on the south side. We decided not to follow him into the tunnel. It was simply too dangerous.

About 10 minutes later, Louie reported Boudin had not appeared. He certainly had not appeared at our end of the tunnel. Perhaps he was just hiding in a recess in the tunnel wall. The police halted all LRT trains from entering from both sides of the tunnel. It was then we started walking south down the tunnel towards the police, who must've been coming north. To hell with the possible danger.

I didn't know this, and I suspect most Calgarians didn't know it either. When the LRT was originally built, there was an offshoot under the Calgary City Hall heading west. At one time, it was proposed that a station be built under the City Hall and so an extension was built, but it had been partially blocked off. I can't imagine that Boudin and, indeed, most Calgarians knew about this, but Boudin was lucky enough to find it.

We turned into the unused extension and noticed that there was a way into the old tunnel. It was pitch black in there. Fortunately, Red had brought a torch. We squeezed through a gap in the wall and entered a long tunnel that disappeared some way off into the darkness. You could also see Boudin's footprints in the dust leading along the tunnel. We assumed that this was a dead end, but we found a metal ladder going up the wall of the tunnel. There was a trapdoor at the end of the ladder. It was open. Boudin had obviously gone this way because when we climbed the ladder we could see that he had emerged in the basement of the City Hall.

I was getting exhausted by this time, but I wasn't going to give up. We could see Boudin's footprints going up the stairs to the main floor. From there, you could see the main entrance of the City Hall. Not that we could see Boudin, but you'd have to bet that he'd gone this way. We were hopefully heading in the right direction. Unfortunately, there was another Covid demonstration enveloping the square outside. There must've been several thousand out there with placards and banners. He could easily lose himself in that throng.

Since we couldn't see Boudin anywhere, we decided it would be better to split up with Red going south, Jen going north, and me going towards the Arts Common block. This was situated just south of the Olympic Plaza and comprised several theatres. I was buggered by now and my run had diminished to nothing more than a fast walk. And then I caught sight of him dashing through the entrance to the Jack Singer Concert Hall. This accommodates about 2,000 people so he could easily get lost in there. I tried to pick up the pace with not much luck, but I could see where he was going. I called Red to help me. There was a symphony concert that night, so there were quite a few people around, despite the limitations prompted by the social distancing legislation.

Boudin went up into the foyer area and then went running up a couple of escalators and up to the top of the building. Why is it that crooks on the run always go to the top of a building, especially when they're being chased by guys like me? Fortunately, he did not consider climbing up to the roof. I'm not even sure there was a way up there.

He made his way to the upper balcony and slid along into one of the private boxes. They would typically house about six people, but they were not being used and had been cordoned off. I think he assumed no one had seen him go in there. But I'd seen where he'd gone. I wasn't sure that I wanted to tackle him on my own. Did he still have the gun?

Fortunately, by this time Red had appeared. We decided to enter the box together. He had no way out. When we got in there, he was standing balanced precariously on the balcony edge. He was not holding a gun. I don't know what he was intending to do, but I suspect he was trying to jump down to the next balcony. It was never going to work. We made a grab for him. He might have jumped or perhaps he slipped or just maybe we had helped him on his way. As he fell, he reached for the balcony railing below, but he bounced off it. He landed on the edge of the stage. It must have been a forty-foot fall. Nobody survives that. Some of the audience screamed, but you could hardly hear them over the orchestra. I was impressed by the orchestra's composure. They kept playing for a little while before it all ground to a halt. I'm sure they don't discuss this at music school. What to do when a body falls on stage. Ironically, the piece they were playing was the Magic Flute, but there would not be any final magic for Boudin..

When we looked down, we could see Boudin's body contorted in death. He had broken his neck. I was tempted to say that this was another situation he simply wasn't able to escape from, but thought better of it. It was just the wrong time. Seconds later, the police and emergency services arrived, and the place was evacuated. In essence, that was it as far as we were concerned on this case. Well, not quite. We had to do a couple of interviews on the radio, but then we slipped away. We sat up late that night. It was not a happy moment. Too many people had died. And what was it all about? Greed, and that's usually the motive in most of these cases.

It had been a fascinating adventure, one that cost me more than I earned. But we had worked together as a team and with an assist from the police, we had solved the case. The day after, we all went to a sweat lodge for what Red described as spiritual healing and to focus on new endeavours. I lasted for about half an hour. Red and Jen endured it for a couple of hours. But we all felt spiritually healed.

24

AFTERMATH

They often say in most tales that they all lived happily ever after and, to a large extent, this was the case. Rita and I stayed together but with a long engagement. We never quite got around to setting a date and, in a way, it didn't matter. She had her ring, and she wore it. People can assume what they want. There was an obvious commitment between us. I told Rita that it would be the last commitment I made. But there were some obvious changes. We both decided to indulge in a healthier lifestyle. I never did check the bird box to see if my cigs were still there. Perhaps the shreds of tobacco had been used to build a nest. We began to do a lot of walking and inevitably, a lot more talking. Our relationship was thriving.

I noted we had considered a healthy lifestyle. I had been warned about my coronary risk for some time and the pains down the left arm were a red light. The docs told me that my heart was in good shape, but I never quite believed them. I'd already had one attack before. I did all the tests, and it was all confirmed. I was, indeed, suffering esophageal reflux. My doctor had been right all along. No, it was not me that caused coronary concerns. It was Rita. She had a slight heart attack one day, but I think as we all know, there is nothing slight about a heart attack. I'd had one before. I knew we would have to change our lifestyle. Between us, I reckoned we lost about 60 pounds over the next few months.

One key to a more stress-free life is cutting down on the obvious stresses. The most obvious for me was my job as a private eye. I wasn't going to give up, but I made a decision that changed things drastically. Red and eventually Jen became a big part of the operation. I had no hesitation in Red becoming a half-partner in Lou Diamond Associates. And Jen was to become a lead investigator, at least for a few months. It all worked. I had the experience; Red had the intelligence and muscle and Jen had just about everything. And when we needed real muscle, there was always Dave. I called him right away.

You might think that the Boudin case had made us famous. I don't think it made much difference. Private investigators don't brag about their successes because there are so many other failures. That's not to suggest that business was bad. It picked up significantly, but not to the extent that Rita and I could consider a house in Pump Hill. I doubt that we would have been welcome there. But the case had one negative effect on me. Watching illusionists just wasn't that much fun anymore. I think I know how they did it.

I know you would like to know about Red and Jen. First, Red. He completed a few more university courses, but the significant change for him was that he became more and more interested in his cultural identity and so did Jen, for that matter. Red discovered more and more about his ancestors and was able to take it a long way back. And then he became interested in politics. Who knows about the future? And yes, they had a wonderful wedding. Red's relatives were all there and Jen's father actually turned up. They are now trying to repair that relationship.

And what about Boudin? He became a footnote in the history of illusions. He was buried at Queens Park Cemetery. There were a few mourners at his burial. I suspect someone will write a biography of him one day. The issue. Will it be found in the Magic and Mystery section or True Crime? Some of his materials had escaped the fire and were sold to another magician. He changed his name from Lenny

Price to Cluedini. Not very imaginative. I think he is still headlining at the Canadian Legion every month.

There was a considerable amount of money left over, and it went to a good cause. We found out that Marie and Boudin had had a child years back they put up for adoption. They had never acknowledged this child. He was to earn a surprising amount of money from parents he had never known.

It was only a few days after the Boudin affair that the next job came in. There had been a mysterious disappearance on the reservation. Would Red be able to help? I thought he could. But it was a baffling case. One of the elders had......Nah, that's another story.

ABOUT THE AUTHOR

DR. ALAN LEBOEUF was born in an industrial city in the north of England and is still proud to call himself a Salfordian. After 18 years he left home for the last time graduating at Sheffield University, Birmingham University and Trinity College, Dublin. Armed with a Ph.D in Clinical Psychology he moved to Bermuda for seven years as a practicing clinician before moving to his present location in Calgary, Alberta where he continued as a psychologist. Apart from his work as a psychologist, he became a correspondent on a local radio show for CBC and also submitted several papers to academic journals. Nine years later he entered the field of theatre taking the lead in a drama with a local community theatre group and then trapped by the acting bug he appeared in 30 plays over the next few years. He wrote his first play in 2012 and since then has written 19 plays, seven of which have been performed. It was 2019 when he bumped into the mythical character of Sidney Arbuckle and this has led to eight books about this character the first of which you see today.

He has now retired as a clinical psychologist but intends to continue to write until the last page. He continues to support various charities and is still passionate about his favourite pastimes. Cricket and rugby.

Some of his accomplishments are listed on the following pages.

Alan hopes you enjoy his work. Feel free to contact him at :
alanl@athabascau.ca.

Full length plays

Those in bold have been produced

Not a leg to stand on (2008): Comedy
Deadly Illusions (2009): Thriller
Eleventh Commandment (2009): Drama
Love on the Ropes (2010): Comedy
Investment in Murder (2012): Thriller
Elvis's Underpants (2015): Comedy
For a Mature Audience Only (2016): Comedy
Unprotected Text (2016): Comedy
The French Kiss Off (2019): Comedy
Just Deserts (2020): Comedy
For services rendered: The Strange Case of John Bodkin Adams (2023): Drama
For an Immature Audience Only (2023): Comedy
Double Dose of Death: Thriller(2025)

One-act plays:

The Student (Radio Play 2013): Thriller
False Flag (2016): Drama
From an unknown source (2019): Drama
Smedley Butler: A Forgotten Hero (2024): Drama

Books.

From the Arbuckle Archives.

Deadly Illusion

Frozen in Fear

Death in the Oilpatch

Outrider

Not a game for gentlemen

Death in Vein.

Kill Shot

Diagnosis Murder

Nothing ventured; nothing gained (an autobiography)

Screenplays

Love on the Ropes

Elvis's Underpants (in preparation)

Thank you for completing *Deadly Illusion.*

We would love if you could help by posting a review at your book retailer and on the PageMaster Publishing site. It only takes a minute and it would really help others by giving them an idea of your experience.

Thanks

PM Store Author's QR Code
https://pagemasterpublishing.ca/by/Alan-LeBoeuf/

To order more copies of this book, find books by other Canadian authors, or make inquiries about publishing your own book, contact PageMaster at:

PageMaster Publication Services Inc.
11340-120 Street, Edmonton, AB T5G 0W5
books@pagemaster.ca
780-425-9303

catalogue and e-commerce store
PageMasterPublishing.ca/Shop

www.ingramcontent.com/pod-product-compliance
Lightning Source LLC
Chambersburg PA
CBHW060930180626
46817CB00004B/1477